TRYST

ELSWYTH THANE was born Helen Elswyth Thane Ricker on May 16, 1900 in Burlington, Iowa, the daughter of a local teacher and high school principal. The family moved to New York City in 1918, and Helen Ricker became Elswyth Thane. She began working as a freelance writer in the 1920s, and became a newspaper writer and a Hollywood screenwriter. Her first novel, *Riders of the Wind*, was published in 1926.

On September 22, 1927, she married 50-year-old naturalist and explorer William Beebe. Beebe died in 1962, leaving only half of his estate to his widow. She lived on the couple's farm in Wilmington, Vermont for the remainder of her life.

Her last work, *Fighting Quaker: Nathaniel Greene*, was published in 1972.

Thane is most famous for her "Williamsburg" series of historical fiction. The seven books cover several generations of several families from the American Revolutionary War to World War II. The action of the books begins in Williamsburg, Virginia and travels to England, New York City, and Richmond, Virginia.

But her most romantic work is *Tryst.*

Elswyth Thane

TRYST

To Order Contact
Aeonian Press Inc.
Box 1200
Mattituck, NY 11952

Reprinted 1974, by
Arrangement with
HAWTHORN BOOKS, INC.

Library of Congress Card Number: 74-4544

To the Reader

It is our pleasure to keep available uncommon titles and to this end, at the time of publication, we have used the best available sources. To aid catalogers and collectors, this title is printed in an edition limited to 300 copies. It has been manufactured in the United States to American Library Association standards on permanent, durable, acid-free paper. ——— **Enjoy!**

The World of

Elswyth Thane

The Williamsburg Novels

Dawn's Early Light
ISBN 0-88411-974-2
Yankee Stranger
ISBN 0-88411-963-7
Ever After
ISBN 0-88411-958-0
The Light Heart
ISBN 0-88411-951-3
Kissing Kin
ISBN 0-88411-970-X
This Was Tomorrow
ISBN 0-88411-962-9
Homing
ISBN 0-88411-969-6

Bird Who Made Good
ISBN 0-8488-1596-3

An engaging departure from Miss Thane's historical themes, this work adds a rare glimse into the personal life of the author.

Bound to Happen
ISBN 0-88411-964-5
Cloth of Gold
ISBN 0-88411-965-3
Echo Answers
ISBN 0-88411-966-1
Family Quarrel
ISBN 0-8488-0726-X
Fighting Quaker: Nathanael Greene
ISBN 0-88411-971-8
From This Day Forward
ISBN 0-88411-960-2
His Elizabeth
ISBN 0-88411-967-X
Letter to a Stranger
ISBN 0-88411-954-8
Lost General
ISBN 0-88411-952-1
Melody
ISBN 0-88411-953-X
Mount Vernon: The Legacy
ISBN 0-88411-959-9
Potomac Squire
ISBN 0-8488-0727-8
Queen's Folly
ISBN 0-88411-955-6
Remember Today
ISBN 0-88411-973-4
Riders of the Wind
ISBN 0-88411-968-8
Strength of the Hills
ISBN 0-88411-961-1
Tryst
ISBN 0-88411-956-4
Tudor Wench
ISBN 0-88411-972-6
Washington's Lady
ISBN 0-88411-957-2

TRYST

I

SABRINA had never picked a lock in her life, but it was done every day in books. She tiptoed along the carpeted upper passage and whisked round the corner to the second flight of stairs leading to the top floor of the house. Gripped tightly in one hand she carried her burglar tools —nail-scissors with curved points, a button-hook, and some wire hairpins stolen from Aunt Effie's dressing-table.

She climbed the stairs stealthily, step by step, and the fine old oak never creaked once under her scant ninety pounds. Sabrina at seventeen had lost her baby fat, but had not yet begun, as Aunt Effie was fond of remarking, to fill out.

At the top of the stairs she stopped to listen, bending perilously double over the bannisters. Not a sound from below. They would think she was reading in her room, which was only natural because it was raining. She was free, reasonably so, till tea time. With a long-drawn breath she faced the locked door, dropped to her knees in front of the keyhole, and set to work.

She bent the hairpins in various ways, patiently. She tried the button-hook from all angles. Then she tried both hairpin and button-hook together. Nothing happened at all, and the small scraping noises she made seemed to reverberate through the tranquil silence of the house. Just as she was about to give up, the hairpin caught and lodged. She exerted cautious pressure with the button-hook. Something gave. Something clicked. She had done it. The lock had turned.

She knelt there, staring at the door, wide-eyed and shaken. The first thing that occurred to her was that now she could never get it locked again. And then she didn't care, for the knob had turned easily under her hand, and the door moved two inches inward. The crack went on widening before her fascinated gaze until, still kneeling, she beheld the forbidden room. With a quick glance behind her at the empty stairs, she snatched up her tools and got to her feet—stepped across the threshold swiftly and closed the door, shutting herself inside.

. . . .

The day they had arrived to take possession of the house, a month ago at the end of March, Sabrina on her early explorations had run up the last flight of stairs because there was that closed door at the top and she naturally wondered what was behind it. To her surprise, when she laid her hand on the knob the door would not open. But they had taken the house—3 reception rooms, 9 bedrooms, 3 bathrooms, electric light, company's gas and water, garage—furnished, by the year.

A locked room. How mysterious. Sabrina at once tried to see through the keyhole, but Aunt Effie called to her from below and told her to come away. There was something in the lease about their not having the use of that room, she said.

Sabrina was asking excited questions over the bannisters such as Why not, and What was in it, and Whose room was it, when she became aware of the housekeeper —a dour middle-aged woman who went with the house, like the furniture, when you let it—standing at the bottom of the stairs looking up at her. Somehow at sight of the woman's still, watchful face the questions died on Sabrina's lips and she came back down the stairs, one foot slowly at a time, towards where Mrs. Pilton stood. And as she reached the bottom—

"That room is kept locked when he's not at home," said Mrs. Pilton in her quiet country voice, and she turned without smiling and went away down the back stairs toward the kitchen. She held herself erect and walked well, a self-respecting woman. More like a governess than a housekeeper, thought Sabrina, making you feel in the wrong when you had done whatever it was quite innocently. With a long backward look up the stairs, she returned to her own room midway of the passage, to unpack.

After that, Sabrina had gone round calling it the Bluebeard Chamber until Father heard and said Nonsense, and explained irritably that the locked room merely belonged to one of the sons who was not available to clear out his possessions from the cupboards and drawers and empty the place for the use of a tenant. Father pointed out that they didn't need the room, just the three of them. Aunt Effie said Mercy, no, the house was too big anyhow. And they both regarded the subject as closed.

Father had retired that winter from his professorship in London, in order to write a book about prehistoric England and those of its highly controversial inhabitants who were responsible for the long barrows, and the mysterious half-obliterated hilltop camps, and the stone circles. The Mendip Hills and surrounding country abound in barrows and stones and ancient mines and encampments, and Father's intention was to live amongst them while he wrote, making excursions by car to neighboring sites when he felt like it, or when the weather was particularly fine, or his desk work palled, or his womenfolk obtruded themselves too much on his notice. Having been without a wife ever since Sabrina was born, Father was not well broken in as regards womenfolk. Aunt Effie and Sabrina bored him, and kept out of his way as much as possible, which only spoilt him and made him the more incompetent to deal with such domestic situations as arose from time to time. But Aunt Effie, who had never been married, believed that all men were pretty much alike. Unless, of course, they were Rakes, she would add. Father wasn't a Rake.

Sabrina's ideas of life were necessarily, in these circumstances, rather constricted, and her experience, compared to that of most girls of her enlightened generation, was calamitously small. Once she had been sent to a fashionable school in Sussex; a very good school, which

Aunt Effie chose by an obscure mental process similar to flipping a coin. The fees were high, the personnel prepossessing, the location healthful and picturesque, and the daily régime quite the thing in girls' schools.

To Sabrina, an only child accustomed either to solitude or to adult society, it was a captivity full of horror. She had to sleep in a room with five other narrow, spartan beds in it, and wash at one of a row of six basins and jugs exactly alike—baths twice a week. The room was lighted after dark by two electric bulbs in white glass shades hung high from the ceiling. She ate at a table for ten among forty-nine other girls. The puddings were heavy, the vegetables were watery, and the lamb was always mutton. In the dining-room the same white light beat down nakedly from above. The pitiless ventilation came from open windows. Strenuous exercise was as inevitable daily as mathematics. Sweets, even if brought from home, were collected by the matron and doled out again on Sundays. Letter-writing was scheduled for two days a week; on other days you had to ask permission to write a letter. If you brought books back with you from holidays at home, they had to be submitted to the Principal. Bells rang all the time, and each one meant you had to stop what you were doing and begin to do something else.

Sensitive, self-contained, old for her years, Sabrina found the detailed supervision of her days wholly fantastic, and considered a good deal of it sheer busybodying on the part of the mistresses. For years at home she had read anything she chose from a large and miscellaneous family library. For years at home it had been assumed that she understood the rudiments of personal hygiene and diet—as for instance, if she ate too many chocolates and then was uncomfortable, it was acknowledged to be her own fault. She was dosed and possibly put to bed, but no one dreamed of confiscating the box. Half the items of the school routine were to her indignities, and most of the others bored her.

Squabbles between sisters, gigglings over boy-friends, half-baked harangues about marriage and careers, passionate cinema crushes—all the normal, cheerful chatter of the dormitory and recreation hours, left her stranded and bewildered, with nothing to contribute. She had no ambition to be a novelist or an actress or an aviatrix or a doctor. She hadn't a secret love affair. She had nothing to boast of, nothing to conceal, nothing to confide. Most of the girls ignored her after a while, and a few of them actively disliked her for a prig or a dolt.

She could not fit in, she did everything out of turn, she was stricken dumb in the classrooms, and failed miserably at games. Every now and then she cried herself sick and begged to go home. She was the problem-child for all time of that very sane and unimaginative school.

Eventually Aunt Effie came and had a mutually confusing interview with the headmistress, who seemed unable to comprehend that Sabrina was only shy, and used to being by herself, and hated gongs, and public ablutions and prayers, and most of all hated competitive games. Then she took Sabrina away—when a whole new term had just been paid for, too—and there was another governess. But governesses, said Aunt Effie, were not what they had been in her day.

The governess was let go when they came to Nuns Farthing, as it would soon be Easter anyhow, and time for a holiday. They had never lived in the country before, because Father needed to be near the British Museum Reading-Room and the University, but in her youth Aunt Effie had been a fervid gardener, and Sabrina was hoping to own a kitten. She did not want a dog, on account of Aunt Effie's Bella, a jealous barrel-shaped fox terrier who got older and crosser and fatter each year, and who in Aunt Effie's eyes could do no wrong.

It was typical of the way Father did things that neither Aunt Effie nor Sabrina had seen the house before they arrived from London prepared to stay in it for an indefinite period of time.

"I have taken a house in the Mendip Hills," said Father one night in London at the end of dinner. "Not far from Dolebury Camp," he added, as though that explained everything.

"To *live* in?" exclaimed Aunt Effie, pardonably surprised, for she had had absolutely no warning.

Father said, though it was really beneath him, that he had no intention of dying in it.

"Well, really, Alan, you might have *told* me! That is, I'd like to have *known!*" Aunt Effie remonstrated.

Father looked at her patiently over his spectacles and pointed out with great reasonableness that she knew now.

"Has it got a garden?" she demanded at once.

Father said Yes, he believed things grew.

"And has it got bathrooms?" persisted Aunt Effie in the order of their importance.

Father set down his after-dinner coffee cup with a small irritable clink.

"My dear Effie," he said, for she was after all his own sister, "there is no reason for you to suppose that I would take a lease on Dolebury Camp itself for a home. The house has three bathrooms, and is otherwise adequately furnished. It is called Nuns Farthing. And don't ask me why," he continued hastily as both their mouths came open, "because I don't know. Wells is the nearest town of any size. I shall be able to use the museum there."

He rose then, and left them, disappearing behind the closed door of his den.

"Men!" said Aunt Effie hopelessly, to the astonished air.

Sabrina was delighted, and began at once to pack.

They arrived at Nuns Farthing by motor with their hand luggage, on a late afternoon in March, with a damp, chilly wind blowing off the Hills.

They had come down the Bath Road from London, with luncheon at Marlborough, and Sabrina had not been so far afield since she was a small child. She had gone a little giddy with a mounting rapture of escape, and freedom, and adventure, brought on by a countryside pregnant with spring and by her own secret conviction that now at last, at last, she was going to live happily forever after. One could never feel sure of that in London, somehow. But from now on she would wake up every morning in the country—in a house, instead of a flat—with a garden outside—with the Hills beyond—with spring coming on. No school. No maimed men singing in the gutters, and hopeless pavement artists with heart-breaking little dogs doing tricks for pennies. No terrifying newspaper contents-bills wherever you looked. No aeroplanes overhead and no nerve-racking traffic underfoot. Nothing but peace and stillness and all this greenness. . . .

When the little car—driven by Aunt Effie, with Sabrina in the rumble seat so that Bella could make herself comfortable in front between Father's feet—turned into the prim, dreaming streets of the Bath suburbs, Sabrina was still excited, still gazing eagerly to right and left, though her eyes had begun to water with the cold and her cheeks were feverish with windburn. She did not mind sitting outside under a rug when the hood was up, because you could see more, even while the wind tangled your upper eyelashes with your lower ones and whipped your hair into wisps and made your ears ache. You hadn't got to listen to people out there, and could think your own thoughts. In her lap under the rug was a book about the Bath Road and coaching days and highwaymen and Beau Nash. She knew it almost by heart, so it didn't matter that she hadn't been able to open it comfortably for reference along the way. The dark tower of the Abbey rose serene and old against the pale March sky—and not having been inside she didn't know how bleak and yet cluttered was its interior, with all those white monuments and tablets.

It was too early for tea, but they stopped at a garage for petrol and when they drove on again she glimpsed the row of Roman Emperors round the top of the Baths, and the place where Bath Oliver biscuits are made—and was amused for several miles because of a sign outside the latter which offered broken bits at a reduced rate per pound.

By that time the Hills began—not bleak and stony as they would have to be round Dolebury, but starred with tree clusters; dipping, rolling, heaving, delicious land, all turning a shy, incredible green. As the road dropped down exquisitely into Wells, the feeling in the pit of Sabrina's stomach had nothing to do with the tired springs of the little car, or with cold, or tea time. She felt all the time now as though one of Selfridge's lifts had plunged downward beneath her, but it was a sensation of sheer excitement and joy.

This was a day she had been coming towards all her life. It would bring the fulfillment of some tremendous, half-dreamed desire. Ugliness and vague fears and unaccountable uncertainty had been left behind, and just ahead, at the end of this day's journey, some still inconceivable enchantment was waiting at the house called Nuns Farthing. I'm coming home, I'm coming home, she told herself over and over again, and had to let it go at that.

Father was chilly and wanted his tea, so they stopped at the Swan in Wells, and went up a flight of carpeted stairs to sit at a table in a window which overlooked the lawn in front of the cathedral. It was a good tea, with strawberry jam and very superior cake, but Sabrina was feeling too odd inside to appreciate it.

"You haven't eaten anything all day," Aunt Effie complained, munching brown bread-and-butter. "At breakfast you were too excited about starting. I'm always a little excited myself about starting somewhere—though it's much worse when one's catching a train, I always think. But we're nearly there now, so you ought to be able to eat something!"

Nearly there. Sabrina rested her eyes on the cathedral beyond its greening lawn—how *motionless* it is, she thought—and wondered at the tingling happiness which sang in her veins.

"Look, Sabrina, chocolate cake!" Aunt Effie urged her. "There's all that unpacking and settling in to be done before dinner time—Alan, don't you think she ought to eat a piece of this lovely chocolate cake?"

But Father's mind was on Wookey Hole, which lay beside the road still ahead of them, northward, along the western rim of the Hills. Prehistoric man had refuged there from Mediterranean invaders. Bones of the mammoth and the bison and the reindeer, to say nothing of the urus, had been found in the caves. There was a museum. Father adored museums. "I supposed it would be foolish to stop there today, just for a swift look round," he said wistfully. Aunt Effie said that it would, and filled his cup for the third time.

Sabrina sat quietly between them, her cheeks aflame from the wind, trying not to choke on the chocolate cake, which was dry and tasteless in her throat. She was not in a hurry—she knew no agonizing need to press on. Whatever it was had been waiting for her a long time, and would still be there when she came. And with this half-formed thought of it, another wave of dizzying sensation surged through her, so that she laid down the cake and fastened her eyes on the cathedral's twin towers for steadiness.

"Well, let's be getting on," said Aunt Effie at last, brushing crumbs out of her tweeded lap. "We've got all summer to see Wells, goodness knows."

It was not a lovely house, at Sabrina's first sight of it, standing gaunt and gray against a barren hillside in the chill early twilight of that March day. Nothing much had been done about the garden, though a few bulbs seemed to be coming up. It was hardly late enough for lights, and the many casement windows watched them blankly as they came round the curve of the drive.

The housekeeper opened the door to them, and remarked that the fires never drew right in that wind. They switched on the electric light and walked about in a somewhat smoky atmosphere with their coats still on, looking hopefully into the strange rooms which enigmatically awaited their scrutiny; comfortably furnished rooms, clothed in chintz and good velour, well lighted and uncluttered with cast-off belongings of the family. Bella sniffed and scrabbled in the corners, and Aunt Effie said it really wasn't bad, and Sabrina—Sabrina shook and shivered like a little racehorse at the post as she crossed the threshold.

Home.

A spacious hall, with a wide oak staircase rising from its middle. Paneled walls, rather gloomy. Two big drawing-rooms, one opening into the garden, and a library which was already Father's own exclusive sacred den. A long dining-room opening off the back of the hall, with family portraits and a cold white marble mantelpiece. The kitchens and so forth lay beyond it. Upstairs, a central passage with rooms off either side. Nine bedrooms. Aunt Effie, popping open doors, muttering busily to herself, efficiently questioning the housekeeper, while Bella pattered at her heels, gave Sabrina her choice of two. The first one had blue-and-white flowered wallpaper and chintzes, a window seat with a long view down the garden in blue twilight, a four-poster bed with chintz hangings—Sabrina drew a long sigh and pulled off her hat and tossed it into the armchair beside the dressing-table. "This is it," she said simply, and for some childish reason she could not understand there was a lump in her throat and she wanted to cry.

"Well, just as you like, dear—Jennie will bring up

your bag in a few minutes. Jennie is the housemaid," said Aunt Effie, and bustled away.

Sabrina walked over and pulled the chain of the bedside lamp, which cast an amber glow across the plump bolster. A book lay on the little table beneath it—just a novel, not very new, but suitable for reading in bed, as though the room had been expecting her. There were more books in built-in shelves beyond the bed. There was a writing-table, stocked with notepaper and pens and ink. Blue glass toilet things. . . . Her room. Waiting for her. With a coal fire grate, and everything laid ready for the match. Her own coal fire in her own room. . . .

Aunt Effie put her head in at the open door.

"You and I will use the bathroom at the end of the passage," she said. "Opposite the upper stairs. Father can have the one next door to the big bedroom, all to himself. That will save trouble," she added darkly. "I'll be just across from you, in the green room. Come, Bella, we'll find a place for your basket now." She vanished again.

It was when she went along the passage to look up the bathroom that Sabrina first noticed the other flight of stairs with that locked door at the top, and was caught peeking. The house, in its spaciousness and dignity and the simple comfort of its furnishings—what Aunt Effie called good value—was perfect in Sabrina's eyes. The exaltation of arrival was subsiding gently into a sense of deep satisfaction, and a healthy fatigue. But the riddle of the locked room was the finishing touch. And the room was actually mentioned in the lease as not being available for use by any possible tenants.

It was not until several weeks had passed that Sabrina began not to be able to stop thinking about the room all day long.

She made a pretext for hunting up Mrs. Pilton, the housekeeper, and then lingered in the passage outside the kitchen.

"By the way," said Sabrina, elaborately casual, "have you got a key to that room—the one that's locked?"

"I have," said Mrs. Pilton.

"Could I see it some time—the room, I mean?"

"There's nothing much to see," said Mrs. Pilton. "He's got his books there, mostly—and the sort of odds and ends a man collects."

"Books?" Sabrina's interest quickened.

"He's a great one to read," admitted Mrs. Pilton.

"So am I," Sabrina informed her eagerly. "I'd like to see his books some time."

"I'm afraid I couldn't let you use them," Mrs. Pilton said firmly. "Even the family never touches his things. He's kept himself to himself, always."

"He sounds very mysterious and rather nice," suggested Sabrina cunningly.

"We don't see so much of him here since he's been grown," said Mrs. Pilton.

"Have you been at Nuns Farthing a long time?"

"Twenty years or more."

"Then you must have known him when he was a child."

"Oh, yes. He and Mr. George were always here for the summer holidays."

"Which of them is the elder?"

"Mr. George."

"Oh. I would like to see the room some time if you're not too busy—"

"I'm afraid not today, I've got the baking to see to."

Sabrina drifted away, feeling baffled. All that, and she had still not learned the name of this evasive creature whose room remained locked and whose things were not touched. Was he the family black sheep, she wondered, and therefore unmentionable? Or was he the jealously guarded darling of them all? Impossible to discover which, from Mrs. Pilton's impassive face and noncommittal replies.

Only a few days after that, Sabrina climbed the upper stairs surreptitiously, to try the key of her own room door in the lock. As she had expected, it refused to turn. And there were books in there that she felt sure she wanted to read. Thoughtfully she returned to her room, and her eyes were caught by a button-hook on the dressing-table, and a small pair of curved scissors. People even picked locks with hairpins. . . . She hadn't any hairpins. But Aunt Effie had.

. . . .

And now at last she stood inside the closed door, full of a pleasant wickedness, and looked about her.

It was a livable, used-looking, comfortable, self-contained room of majestic proportions, with nothing of the garret about it. It was essentially a private room, for he was a man who kept himself to himself. It looked to her eager eyes as though it expected him to walk back into it at any minute.

But Sabrina, who was shy of strangers, was not at all disturbed by the off-chance of being caught by him in the very act of trespassing. She was so sure, as soon as she saw the room, that it was expecting her too.

It was L-shaped, for a wall had been knocked out between two smaller rooms. From the door you faced the large carved oak mantelpiece, with a modern chintz-covered chesterfield at right angles to it, and a smoking-table with a lamp and ashtray at its right hand. The wall on your left and the space either side of the mantelpiece was filled with open bookshelves. Opposite the chesterfield the wall, which ran the length of both rooms, had two casement windows opening above the garden to the south, with a cushioned window seat beneath each of them, and the ceiling, though high, revealed the slope of two gables. The big, practical knee-hole desk stood at an angle to the near window. This, with a couple of chintz armchairs and the low fireside hassock, made the living-room end.

In the L to your right was the other window, with a tall chest of drawers beyond. The bed, an enormous square without a footboard, covered with wine-colored velour and heaped with dark silk cushions, stood with its head against the middle of the end wall, on one side of it a table with a reading-lamp and some books, on the other a door. Against the right-hand wall was a splendid mahogany wardrobe. There was a low chair under the casement window, and an old chest at the end of the bed. The rugs were soft, faded Persians.

Sabrina was irresistibly drawn to the nearest bookcase. . . .

The fading of the short spring day, when the page gradually got too dim to be read without a light, reminded her that she would be missed from downstairs as tea time came on. She unfolded herself from the chesterfield, replaced the book on the shelf, and started hastily downstairs.

At the bottom of the upper flight Mrs. Pilton stood, her hand on the newel-post—waiting. Sabrina went scarlet, and caught at the bannister.

"I—wanted to see the books," she said limply.

"You've been inside," said Mrs. Pilton. Her eyes were searching, but not unfriendly.

"I'm afraid I picked the lock," confessed Sabrina. "With a hairpin and a button-hook."

"You knew I had a key," said the woman, immovable.

"I knew you wouldn't lend it to me." Sabrina hurried down the last few steps and laid an impulsive hand on Mrs. Pilton's sleeve. "Please don't lock the door again!" she begged. "Please let me go in sometimes! I won't do any harm. I'll only take out one book at a time, and I'll always put it back exactly where I found it. Surely he wouldn't mind my going into his room, if I'm very careful not to disturb anything?"

The woman looked down at her remotely, without smiling, and Sabrina took her hand off the black-clad arm and fell back a step.

"I—I'm sorry," she faltered. "I knew it was wrong, but I—didn't mean to pry—" Her eyes filled with tears. "It's much the nicest room in the house," she added in her own defense, and turned away blindly towards her bedroom further down the passage.

"If you feel that way about it," the woman's quiet voice came after her, "I'll leave the door as it is."

Sabrina swung round incredulously to thank her, and saw only Mrs. Pilton's back, receding towards the servants' stairs, her shoulders erect and uncompromising as usual.

For several weeks Sabrina and Mrs. Pilton shared the secret between them. But an afternoon naturally had to come when Aunt Effie called and got no reply, went to Sabrina's room and found it empty, called again, urgently, and was answered at last by a very small voice from the top floor.

Aunt Effie was aghast. Leases were leases, and there was a clause. If the intrusion were known, they could be forced to leave the house. She stood halfway up the stairs, arguing, while Sabrina hung on to the bannister at the top, defending herself tearfully and maintaining that it was only for the books, and that she did nobody any harm by reading them and putting them back.

In the midst of it Mrs. Pilton's low-pitched voice came up to them from the passage.

"I don't think there'd be any objection," she was saying, "so long as she takes nothing out of the room."

"Did you know she had got into it?" demanded Aunt Effie, astonished.

"Yes, I knew," said the housekeeper.

"You should have told me at once," scolded Aunt Effie. "I could have put a stop to it."

Mrs. Pilton's eyes rested a moment on Sabrina's flushed and anxious face.

"I was willing to take the responsibility," she said, and went away.

But Aunt Effie was not. She ordered Sabrina to close the door at once and come down. She threatened to speak to Father about it. She enlarged on dreadful speculations as to what the family would say to this violation of the sacred terms of the lease.

Sabrina listened meekly, and the next afternoon while Aunt Effie drove into Wells for some shopping, Sabrina set her square little jaw and went back to the top floor room.

So, with Father still in ignorance, Aunt Effie deceived, and Mrs. Pilton looking the other way, her visits to the secret sanctuary continued, until she knew the room and its visible contents by heart. Sometimes it almost seemed as though she knew its owner too. Sometimes it was almost as though he himself was there in the room—waiting for her to come back to him. His dominant masculine personality which had put its imprint on his room was a thing almost tangible, as real as the persistent odor of good tobacco which clung about the worn brown pipe he had left behind on the desk.

In the beginning she kept to the middle of the road, as it were, and her invasions were made more or less on tiptoe. She would take a book from the shelf, carry it to the upholstered window seat where the sun fell warmly through the glass, and there, curled up among the cushions, sometimes with an extra one laid across her long silk legs for warmth, she would read, for as long as she dared be absent from below stairs. And then she would replace the cushions, return the book to the shelf, and with a last look round to make sure everything was exactly as she found it, she would steal away.

There were favorites of her own in his library, and hundreds of unknowns she meant to read. If he liked an author at all, he apparently never rested till he had got hold of everything that had ever been printed by him or her. The set was often miscellaneous, bought all at different times. But out-of-print early works had been tirelessly run down, and new ones purchased as they appeared, so that of contemporary writers whose first volumes were immensely vital and full of talent and have now become hard to get, the room was a gold-mine. She began to appreciate that priceless vein of pre-war literature, produced in an incredibly tranquil world where motor cars were still a luxury and aeroplanes almost undreamt of, when taxes and death duties were paid without tragic ruination, and when a comparatively prosperous peasantry relied on the paternal indulgence of a comparatively solvent squirarchy. It was a fascinating world, as remote to one whose memory went no further back than the General Strike as were the days of the Reform Bill or the Regency.

But she had learned as time went on that the room was full of distractions. Her eyes would wander from the page to the mantelpiece or the top of the desk, or the great chest of drawers, or to the wall beyond the wardrobe where some framed pictures hung, or to the door beside the head of the bed—where did it lead?—what hung behind the carved panels of the wardrobe?—what was beneath the lid of the old oak chest? In the desk drawers there must be letters addressed to him, whose envelopes—one would of course never think of looking beyond the envelopes—would reveal the provoking secret of his first name. The family name was Shenstone, everyone knew that, and he had a brother George, but he somehow preserved without effort his own exasperating anonymity.

Could one look closely at the pictures on the wall, without prying? Could one tell by his clothes, if any still remained in the wardrobe, what sort and size of man he was? There must be clues on the mantelpiece and on the desk—clues to the absorbing personality which had made this place its home, and which still pervaded the atmosphere like inaudible music. So much of him was here, under her hand, for the taking. Would it be an unpardonable sin to try to know him a little better?

She was sure that it would. And yet she could no longer resist the attempt. She had to know more about him. Most of all, she had to know his age, his name, and what he looked like. You couldn't go on being a person's guest for weeks and not know what his intimates called him, nor how to recognize him if he—well, if he suddenly walked in the door.

That idea began to bewitch her, with all its infinite possibilities—the idea of his unexpected return. She dwelt on it even when she wasn't in the room, and it made her absent-minded at luncheon and deaf when she wandered alone in the garden, wondering what he would think of Aunt Effie's innovations there.

A solitary child among people of no imagination, Sabrina had always invented and played her own games. Gradually this mysterious Mr. Shenstone was turning into the newest and most tantalizing game she had ever had, superseding all the others. It was a sort of treasure hunt, she told herself, and when you had got together enough pieces you would have assembled a complete person.

One couldn't visualize him clearly, of course, he was just a vague tweed shape, a nice voice, and quiet laughter. His age was the first problem, perhaps, to be solved, and for that there was Mrs. Pilton's evidence. Mrs. Pilton had been with the family twenty years, she said, or more. Then twenty years ago he must have been a child, which meant that he couldn't be much more than thirty now. Nor much less, either, because he was out in the world somewhere on his own. They hadn't seen much of him here since he was grown, Mrs. Pilton said. George was older. How old was George?

She was sure that if Mr. Shenstone returned—it had begun almost to be *when* he returned—he not only would not mind that she had been reading his books, but would urge her to enjoy them all, as quickly as possible, because that was what books like his were for. Most of them were well worn, and looked very traveled. There were odd stains and injuries to their bindings. Some of them appeared to have been chewed by mice or beetles. Some had got wet. It was hardly possible for books which had remained all their lives at Nuns Farthing to look like that, unless he had slung them round the garden and dropped them in the bath.

If he came back, that would be one of the first questions she would ask him—What *have* you done to your poor books? Perhaps if he came back she would learn why *Kim* was discolored with what looked like strong tea, and why *The Gods of Pegana* was freckled with something like mildew, and why the green cloth covers of *Jungle Peace* were minutely gnawed in patches till each separate thread stood bare of varnish.

Being one of the family, he would doubtless show her round the property a bit—if he came back—and perhaps even reminisce of his boyhood here in the house. They would have tea under the big tree on the lawn and she would pour out for him from the old silver service which his mother must have used when he was a child. And miraculously Father and Aunt Effie would always be occupied, so that she had him entirely to herself. . . .

At this point the game would sort of bog down in his inevitable formlessness. If he came back—yes. But where would he come back from? What did he do while he was away? Where was he now? What would he look like? What did his brother call him?

Treasure hunt.

The decision to try and find him somehow in his room was made at last, on another rainy day early in June when Aunt Effie was going to the local sewing circle, and Sabrina would have the rest of the afternoon to herself. It was only part of the game, to try to guess at him through the things he had lived among. And surely he wouldn't have left anything too intimate lying about in plain sight. She would only look at the things any housemaid with a duster could have seen—things she could inspect without lifting or touching. She would keep her hands behind her the whole time. . . .

Each escape into the sanctuary was always an adventure, but this time she closed the door behind her and stood with her back against it, gazing at the room with a new excitement, wondering where to begin. The rain came down soundlessly outside, the streaming window panes blotting out the extraneous world. And in the room it was almost as though he watched her, amused by his incognito, waiting for her to make the first move, willing to be discovered if she was clever enough.

Uncertainly she went to the hearthrug and stood there looking up at the objects on the mantelpiece, her hands behind her back. Surely there must be an inscription, a signature, somewhere, recognizable as his. Recognizable how? She drew nearer the mantelpiece. That large blue porcelain jar—potpourri? Her itching fingers succumbed to temptation. Gingerly she lifted the lid and stood on tiptoe—tobacco! She dipped exploring fingertips and held the crisp brown shreds to her nose—a clean, exciting, mannish smell which was new to her. Father smoked cigars.

She replaced the lid of the tobacco-jar soundlessly, and moved on to her right. The tall ivory carving came next, in which the sail of a Chinese fishing-boat followed the natural bend of the tusk in an oddly logical curve—a fragile, priceless piece, yellow with age. Those candlesticks—massive Georgian silver—family candlesticks, or else he liked the weight and sheen of them—the room could be lighted by electricity. No clock on the mantelpiece. No clock anywhere. That was one reason for the timeless serenity of the room. There was no stopped clock in it to make it seem dead, and no busy ticking to remind one of meals and obligations below stairs. Then he must depend on a watch. Probably a wrist watch. Score one to the mantelpiece.

The flowered chintz which covered the chairs and window seat was the same as the curtains at both windows, and it was not new—so the room had all been done over at the same time, as a whole, by the same person. (Elementary, my dear Watson! Sabrina was enjoying herself.) The desk stood where the sun from the south would fall across the shoulders of the person who sat there, the light coming properly from the left. Child of an habitual desk-worker who was fussy about his light, Sabrina deduced that the owner of the desk must use it a good deal. Did he perhaps write books, like Father? A thorough search of his own shelves might catch him there.

It was a spacious, workman-like desk, with rows of drawers either side of the knee-hole, and on its broad surface a book-blotter and a silver inkwell, with a few enticing small objects round the edges, such as an ivory carving of a mermaid with her tail pulled round under her chin. There was also a very modern fountain-pen in an onyx desk-stand. Father still preferred fine steel nibs.

How long since that fountain-pen had been used? Again her fingers itched. She lifted the pen from its holder and tried it on the blank side of the desk-calendar engagement-pad. The pen was quite dry, of course, and the calendar presented its large black figures for evidence: *June 5, 1936.*

For a moment she stared at it, paralyzed by the coincidence—for today was the fifth of June too. He had last turned the date leaf of that calendar exactly two years ago today. She told herself at once that it was no good feeling creepy about a thing like that, nor was it any wonder that everything had got so dusty. But still—it *was* a coincidence.

On the far corner of the desk were book-ends modeled from the Sphinx's head, holding between them a dictionary, a thesaurus, a Hindu grammar, Kipling's collected verse, and a cross-word puzzle book. Was this strange assortment what he wanted oftenest? A Hindu grammar—Kipling—Asia—the ivory carvings—and the sphinxes—that all hung together. He traveled. He had been out East. His books went with him. That made sense.

She slid out the puzzle book and opened it. He had solved them methodically about halfway through the volume, and a glance at the clues told her they were difficult ones. All her good resolutions about not touching anything forgotten now in the thrill of the chase, she put the book back and lifted one of the sphinxes. A small label pasted on the underside of its base bore a foreign name and *Cairo*. He must have been to Egypt. . . .

For a moment the sphinx, held at an angle between her hands, regarded her calmly, and the corners of its mouth seemed ever so slightly indented in a smile. "You could tell me everything, if you only would," she rebuked it aloud, and set it down again with a lingering hand.

He had left the room so suddenly, or had been so sure that he was coming back soon, that his pipe still lay beside a tobacco pouch at the edge of the blotter, and there was still burnt-out tobacco in the bowl. She picked up the pipe and sniffed it daintily, and then held it a moment in her hand, liking the feel of the smooth brown wood. One of the man's most cherished and intimate possessions, it drew a sense of his very presence all about her, till she half expected the touch of his hand on her shoulder, or the sound of his voice at the door. Reluctantly, she laid it down exactly as it had been. Of all the things he had left behind, it looked loneliest, and forlorn.

There was one thing more she wanted to do before she left the desk. Its closed drawers were of course inviolate. But the book-blotter—people sometimes left letters in a blotter like this one—it had a lid of simple tooled leather—if there should be just an envelope addressed to him . . .

With cautious fingertips she raised the lid, and let it fall again, with a guilty glance over her shoulder. There was something in the blotter. The sphinx seemed to be watching her with its wise near-smile.

Defiantly once more she lifted the lid of the blotter and it dropped back open, exposing a closely written sheet with a signature, and another unfinished page which must be his reply, in his own handwriting. The letter written to him began: *My dear Shenstone*—and was signed *Walter Thompson.* The letter he had begun in reply to *My dear Thompson* was dated June 5, 1936—and had never got as far as a signature.

Sabrina scowled down at it with vexation. It was as

though he was determined to thwart her. It was as though he teased her willfully.

A glance at the waste paper basket showed that it had been emptied, and Thompson's envelope was gone. Defeat. . . .

II

—WITH rifles and ammunition, ready to move within a week's time. The Mullah was at X, the stores at Y. Dalton knows the rest.

He signed his name and the date with a very unsteady hand—*Hilary Shenstone, June 5, 1938*—on the last of those precious pages; figures and diagrams and a hasty map in pencil on a few smudged leaves torn from a pocket notebook. And a hot wind scattered sand across the ink as it dried.

The plane lay on its back, shining in the desert glare. Two long skid marks led up to it, deepening towards the spot where it had finally dug its nose into the sandy ground and somersaulted. Its trim military lines showed little damage except for a crumpled wing-tip. In its protecting shadow Hilary lay propped against the bundle of an unused parachute. He wore an ordinary civilian khaki shirt and shorts. His left side from above the waist downward was caked in his own blood round the bandage on a two days old bullet wound, and his breathing had become difficult. He reached for his khaki coat on the ground beside him, and began to go through its pockets methodically.

A silver cigarette-case and lighter, which he laid across his signature as a paper-weight; a bunch of keys, a pocket-knife and a bottle-opener, a nail-file, a handful of coins, a compass, a small leather-bound engagement-book, a tin box of peppermints, a pipe and tobacco pouch—he came at last to his wallet and its few papers. Two thin letters with English air-mail stamps he laid to one side. A three-cornered butterfly-envelope made of a ruled notebook page came next, labeled *Roadside near Kohat—Junonia*, and enfolding a male of that species destined for his small and very exclusive collection at home; a youthful habit he had never outgrown was the acquisition on every job of some such exquisite trophy, each one a separate jewel of memory. A picture cut out of the *Tatler* was next—a fair girl in her presentation gown and feathers. With only a brief glance he placed it on the letters, his eyes caught and held by the snapshot which was beneath it, and which showed a curving drive shaded by old trees, leading to a stone house with pointed gables and rows of casement windows. The edge of a well-kept lawn was visible, and flowers bloomed. And yet the house stood somehow barren and bleak, with a bare hillside rising behind it.

He had not been there for two years. On the top floor in a long, L-shaped room was all his boyhood. Not a very luxurious room, furnished with odds and ends left over from downstairs. But the casement windows opened above the garden to the south, the armchairs were comfortable, his desk was Chippendale, and the mantelpiece, displaced from the drawing-room a hundred years ago by a vulgar piece of Victorian marble, was Jacobean oak. Not a very luxurious boyhood either, if it came to that, shadowed by the Great War, and dominated by the ruthless, abiding knowledge of what was expected of him when he grew up.

He stared down at the snapshot, his teeth clenched against the flood-tide of emotion which took him unawares at sight of it. He was not often homesick, not since his Spartan schooldays had imposed an agony of longing for the privacy and solitude of that gable room. And for the past ten years, at least, he had been pretty busy, all over the world, wherever his job took him.

He had missed England, of course—missed the serene, unhurried, green-clad background of the cool English countryside, where it is still possible to forget that the twentieth century has got a bit out of hand, and to conceive a world miraculously empty of machines. And sometimes he had thought of England with a kind of gratitude, or rather a thanksgiving that such a place still existed in a complicated modern world—a place where a man's home was still more or less his castle, where a people with jolly, unfurtive faces still lined the curbs to cheer a smiling, friendly ruler who was still His Majesty, and where spring still came so sweetly in secluded lanes and unregimented villages.

Often and often he had thought of England, when he was half across the world—tenderly, as a man may think of his mother, striving in his small and solitary way to keep her safe as she was, protected, and provided for. Oh, yes, he thought of England. . . . In Egypt once, when he had sought out the Sphinx for company, and derived a solemn sort of comfort from its vast immemorial loneliness; in China, where the heat and smells and miserable millions of passive mankind had set him pondering on things it is no good thinking about. . . . But he had never before experienced anything like the persistent nostalgia which had begun to dog him recently, drawing him back, not just to England, but to that gaunt house in the Mendips.

True, he had left it in a great hurry, at a sudden call from the Home Office. He had not stopped to put anything away in his room at the top of the house. His country clothes were left hanging in the wardrobe, his books were strewn about, he had not even locked up his letters and papers. Worst of all, he had left his favorite pipe behind.

He tried to suppose that this was what worried him, and why he felt such a nagging need to return. This, and some subconscious premonition that today was coming; his wound, the crash, and now the final check-up of his belongings and affairs. He should not have left home in such a hurry. It was untidy and careless and not like him. But the Home Office had been urgent on the telephone and he had packed an overnight bag and caught the London train from Wells in less than thirty minutes. It was only for a conference, they said. But in less than thirty hours he was crossing the Channel in an India Mail plane. That was June, 1936, and since then one thing had led to another for two years.

He must get back home. But why? His mind fumbled over it futilely for the hundredth time, and he wondered if fever was making him muzzy. But as for that, the unreasoning desire to return home had begun to torment him weeks before he got the wound. As much as four or five months ago, it had begun. And even then, he was never able to account for it, though it was so strong then that he had been tempted to throw up everything and take the first boat out of Calcutta. Half hunch, half dream, the thing would not down. Against his will he had allowed himself to be talked out of it by a worried high commissioner with an almost impossible job to be done. The impossible always appealed to Hilary because people looked so silly when he did it after all. He listened, he asked questions, he thought he saw a way—and so for the first time in his life he turned his back on a hunch, because it said "Go home!" and India said "Go on!"

His own instructions, telephoned back from London that June day to Mrs. Pilton, had been to lock up his room just as it stood, until his return. Not that it contained any such commonplace embarrassments as indiscreet correspondence or diaries. Keepsakes, yes, most of them untranslatable to the uninitiated, perhaps. Things he valued for their associations, like his butterflies and beetles pinned in their neat insect boxes; his stamp albums, lovingly toiled over for years past in childhood holidays; a few pressed plants in crumbling blotters—he had never quite got the hang of that. No birds' eggs, no pop-gun victims. But a record for anyone to read of a boy's eternal bower-bird instinct to accumulate and to hoard. Things he had lived with all his life. Bits and pieces of himself, which he would have given decent burial if he could have foreseen today. At least he should have taken time to supervise the dust-sheets as usual. He should have locked the door, and put the key in his pocket. But he had not expected to be away so long, nor to come so far. . . .

A puff of hot desert air lifted the *Tatler* cutting and tumbled it away along the ground and into the furrow beside the half-buried engine. The pilot gave up trying to crawl back into the cockpit upside down and turned, a very lightweight canteen dangling by its strap from his hand. Gravely he retrieved the bit of paper from the ground and carried it towards its owner. Except for a slight limp from a banged kneecap, the pilot was uninjured. It was notable that he wore the uniform of a wing-commander.

"The Honorable Alice is a long way from home," he remarked casually, replacing her beside the letters on the coat.

Hilary Shenstone pinned her down with the compass and glanced up at the tall figure beside him.

"I'm feeling the least little bit in the world homesick myself," he admitted.

The pilot offered him the canteen in silence. Hilary shook it questioningly and hesitated.

"There's another one in the plane," lied the pilot, and watched while the wounded man took a long, grateful swallow.

With fingers that were no longer steady, Hilary gathered up his keys and the penciled pages he had signed.

"You take charge of these," he said. "Pearson wants them badly at Peshawur."

"Then he'd better come and get them," said the pilot cheerfully. "We're staying here, my lad."

"You too?"

"Me too," he nodded, looking up at the crippled machine. "If Pearson sends after us they'll sight the plane. And I think he'll send after us." He sat down beside the parachute bundle, in the shade of the mighty wing. "We're very valuable people," he added, and grinned.

"One of us is damaged," remarked Hilary, with a glance at his wound. "You'll have to write my family, Bill. You'll hate that, won't you!"

"How do you know I'll have to?" objected the other man, and his eyes went up to the empty, brassy sky. "The postal service round here is none too good just now."

They sat for a long minute in silence, so that the rustle of dry tufts of grass in the hot wind was audible. But the sound their ears were subconsciously attuned to, the hum of a distant plane, was absent.

"Homesick, are you," said Wing-Commander Dalton at last. "And what part of England belongs to you?"

"Well, there's that bit there." Hilary handed him the picture of the gray house with the hills beyond. "In the Mendips."

"Mendips, eh," said Dalton. "That's a weird piece of country. I'm from Buckinghamshire, myself. Up Amersham way."

"Tidy," conceded Hilary. "Good ale, in those parts. Yes, the Mendips are weird. And the house itself is a bit grim. I liked it when I was a kid, though. It will never be mine, of course, I'm the younger son." He said it simply, without bitterness, and shifted painfully against his lumpy pillow. "This was to be my last job for a while. I was going home the end of this month."

Dalton moved nearer to him and shoved the bundle aside so that Hilary was supported more comfortably against his shoulder.

"We'll get you home, old boy," he said gently. "Give us time. We'll see to it." He glanced again at the empty sky.

"No time," said Hilary faintly, and his unsteady fingers began to pick aimlessly at the edge of the wallet where it lay. "No time now—too far to Waterloo—now—"

"Good old Waterloo," said Dalton.

"You get out of the train," Hilary went on wistfully, and his eyes, half-closed against the desert glare, saw again the cool dim murk of the railway station, the shabby guard in a peaked cap, the ambling, underfed-looking porters, the unhurried flow of the crowd towards the barrier, "and you watch your stuff come out of the van, and you get it on to a taxi—"

"And you get one of those taxis driven by a nice old bloke who thinks he's still got a horse-cab," put in Dalton.

"—and you find yourself crossing the Bridge, and there's Westminster on the left, and the Embankment—and you go on past the Needle and the sphinxes to Charing Cross— You know, that time I came home from Egypt I'd almost forgotten we had those sphinxes on the Embankment—gave me quite a shock to see them sitting there smiling, when I'd just left the original—"

"They do smile, that's a fact," said Dalton, as though it had just occurred to him for the first time. "Bit smug, they are—as though they knew all the answers."

"—and then after Charing Cross you keep on past the Carlton—and there's the club—" Hilary sighed the long sigh of a tired child whose day is done, and turned his head against Dalton's shoulder so that his face was shielded from the hot glare beyond the narrow shadow of the plane's wing. "I haven't forgotten," he said with satisfaction. "I haven't forgotten an inch of the way—I could do it in my sleep—I know the way home so well—"

"But you've only got us as far as the club, old boy," Dalton objected mildly. His arms were aching with the sagging weight of the wounded man, but his voice was low and soothing. The crash had opened the wound again, the slow red stain was spreading, and there was nothing to do but wait, and keep him talking, keep him homesick and drowsy and patient, as long as possible. "The club's not home, after all—"

"*London's* home," Hilary broke in fretfully. "*England's* home. Anywhere in England will do," he insisted, battling the strange new, unreasonable, insurgent knowledge that for him the journey was not ended, could never end again until that spare gray house in the Mendips was reached. "Don't split hairs, Bill—"

"But how about that house—the one you've got a picture of—"

"I was only trying out a new camera. The house stood there, so I snapped it. I'm not sentimental about it," he assured himself for the hundredth time. "It's an ugly house, Bill—the garden is good, though—"

"I can see that, in the picture. How do we get to the Mendips from the club, old boy?" persisted Dalton kindly.

"We spend the night at the club," Hilary explained, his dimming mind tricked and held by the other man's merciful game. "They'll try to get us to stay in Park Street—that's where mother's town house is—but we'll tell 'em we have to report to the Home Office. They can't argue with the Home Office. It's the best friend I have in the world. After dinner—we'll have to have dinner with the family, you know—but after dinner we'll go back to the club and have another hot bath and then read in bed—*all* the new magazines and papers—stacks of them. And then in the morning directly after breakfast we'll take the train from Paddington—and we'll be home in time for lunch. It's a queer sort of place, you know, with a queer name. It's called Nuns Farthing. Mother won't live in it since my father died, and George—that's my brother—George says it gives him the pip. They always threaten to let it, but nobody wants a place like that any more. You can't keep maids because it's too far from a cinema. There's a housekeeper. She keeps it going when the family's away. Mrs. Pilton will look after us. We'll spend the night. There's something I've got to do there—my old room is on the top floor—I left things strewn about, rather—I thought I was going back—it's two years this month—I meant to go home—just lately it's got terribly important to me to get back—I'm not very clear—I'll know when I get there—something to look after—I don't know why, but I *must* go back there before I die—"

"Of course you'll go back, old boy! You leave it to us—little old R.A.F. We'll get you back!" Dalton drew his numbing arms tighter round the spent body they supported, and his eyes swept the empty white-hot sky again, hopelessly.

He was never one to ask questions, but he found himself wondering now about the man who was fast slipping into unconsciousness in his hold; this young, level-eyed, unobtrusive man with the very quiet voice—not much past thirty—who without even writing C.I.D. after his name was understood to have brought off some of the most ticklish jobs in the United Kingdom—well, yes, a secret agent if you put it that way—very highly thought of at the Home Office—knew dialects—knew natives—always knew, they said at Peshawur, where the corpse was hidden. Pearson was crazy, letting him start out alone this time. Well, Pearson had found that out, a bit late, and sent after him—sent one fairly good wing-commander in a small pursuit plane, instead of an army transport with a few good fellows carrying rifles. Less conspicuous, said Pearson. Quite so. But of course there was shooting and this irreplaceable man was hit. And then there was a spot of crawling among the rocks after dark to get back to the plane. And then the plane had been tampered with. Well, it must have been, there was no one to guard it while he went into the village, and the engine came over all queer after an hour's flying. Anyway it had got them out of the neighborhood, they weren't being shot at any more—not yet, that is. Younger son, was he—and George sat soft at home and inherited. Well, that was the way it went. About the Honorable Alice, now—where did she come in. . . .

"Bill, am I out of my head?"

"No, of course not. No more than I am."

"The date, Bill—I've lost track of things—it *is* the fifth of June, 1936?"

"1938, old boy."

" '38, yes, of course—what did I say?"

"We both had a bit of a jolt, you know—"

"1938," repeated Hilary. "Certainly. For a minute I

wasn't quite sure—it was a nasty feeling, suddenly not to be sure of the date—as if I was floating in time—things have begun to slip, Bill—"

"You're making sense, all right. You're telling me about that house of yours in the Mendips. How did it get its funny name?"

"Nobody knows. It's on the foundations of a nunnery, of course— Bill, are you much good at praying?"

"Not very much, I'm afraid."

"Those nuns, Bill—they'd know how—they weren't ashamed of anything they'd done—well, neither am I—" His voice caught sharply in his throat and struggled on again. "It's hard to know how to say it—but—oh, God, if I've earned heaven when I die, let me have England first—let me have England *instead*—"

III

. . . SABRINA closed the blotter and moved on slowly, away from the desk and into the bedroom end, where she had never ventured before.

On top of the chest of drawers was a silver frame enclosing the picture of a fair girl in her presentation gown and feathers. She was very nearly a great beauty, but her mouth was thin and at the same time pouting. Spoilt, thought Sabrina, regarding her with a mixture of surprise and hostility. *With Love, ALICE* was written across one corner of the picture. Alice too was in the absurd conspiracy to withhold his name. Who was Alice?

Beside the picture was a round leather box, with its catch hanging loose. Between two fingers Sabrina lifted the lid. It was full of winged collars for evening wear. Did he dress for dinner every night in the country? In the center space lay something small and black and cold, like a snake. Sabrina looked again, incredulously—yes, it was—nestled in the stiff, encircling collars lay a peculiarly deadly-looking revolver.

Sabrina lifted down the collar box and held it to the light, staring at the gun. It was the first one she had ever seen, close like this, and her heart was beating thickly.

It was somehow wholly terrifying to come upon a gun so casually, as though he thought nothing of it at all, to toss it in among his dress collars. Or did he like to keep it handy? Was it loaded? She sensed that it was ready for business at a touch on the trigger. Why did he have a gun, here in his room? Such a compact, efficient, up-to-date-looking gun, too, surely the very latest thing in sudden death. And yet so small.

The box was heavy in her hands with the gun's weight. She picked the thing up between her thumb and fore-finger, holding it by the extreme end of its handle. How heavy it was, and how cold to the touch. But so small that in a man's hand, held closely in his palm, it would be scarcely noticeable. Very gently she laid it back in its nest among the collars, and replaced the box beside Alice. They were odd companions.

She felt shaken and sobered by the encounter with the gun. She had been in the same room with it day after day, and she might never have known it was there. Didn't he need it, wherever he was now? Had he got another? He had been out East, yes—and men carried guns as a matter of course in India and China these days. So if he had gone back there, why hadn't he taken it with him? Where was he now, and why a gun, loaded and ready to fire, living in his room?

She backed away from the chest of drawers slowly until she backed into the bed.

The table beside the bed held books and a lamp, and an ashtray. Sabrina was strangely reassured at sight of them. He was an entirely rightminded person anyway. He read in bed. She rounded the foot of the bed and approached the door in the wall on the other side, pulled it open a few inches and peeked in. A small bathroom, modern and complete, lighted by a narrow window, with a gay oiled silk shower curtain and a gay linoleum underfoot. He had let himself go, there. She withdrew from the bathroom, a little startled, and found the group of pictures on her immediate right.

She turned to them, but not hopefully, for a man wouldn't put up his own picture in his own room. There was a middle-aged soldier in khaki, with a lot of gold braid on his cap—a colonel at least, she decided, possibly a general—she had no experience in soldiers. It was a thin, kindly, humorous face, with wide dark eyes and a strong, beautiful mouth under the small military mustache. Perhaps his father? And if so, was there possibly a resemblance? Was he a soldier too? Somehow she hoped not. Somehow she was almost sure that he was not.

Next there was a large photograph of a snowy mountain peak—she had no way of knowing it for Everest with his eternal plume. Next, another photograph of a yacht under full sail—perhaps the old King's *Britannia* —sky, wind, and water, and the leaning sail. Last, a group of boys in football suits, seated on a lawn. Boys about twelve or fourteen years old. She bent closer. He must be there among them if only she knew which one he was. For a long time she stared at the picture. At last she turned away with a sigh of frustration, and was facing the wardrobe.

But that would be as bad as opening desk drawers, and she had promised herself not to go as far as that. That would be unpardonable prying.

Her eyes rested wistfully on the carved panels. Somewhere along the way the game had turned into deadly earnest. The owner of the room was no longer an exhilarating sort of jigsaw puzzle. He had become a person, somebody she desperately needed to find. Perhaps it was the gun. Perhaps it was his gay and entirely practical bathroom. Perhaps it was the picture of solemn little boys with a football, which held his childhood. Something had suddenly made him real, a human being, a man who smoked a pipe and read in bed—a man one could talk to and laugh with and depend on if one got frightened. Father didn't count. Father was out of date and out of touch with the world. Aunt Effie didn't count either. Aunt Effie was never frightened. That is, not about anything that mattered. But this man, who was still young, though he was used to guns, and had perhaps even seen the Sphinx face to face, and had read nearly everything—he could explain things, he could answer questions, and yet surely he could still remember the time when he too had wanted to know. . . .

Her hand was on the latch of the wardrobe. A coat or two—possibly riding-clothes—a mackintosh—why should she want to see them? Men's clothes were all alike. . . .

One panel swung out toward her, then the other.

Exactly the sort of thing Father wore. Only—she lifted a coat sleeve and rubbed her fingers across it like a caress—for all its rough weave it was surprisingly soft. And from it came the faint, unmistakable scent of pipe smoke. She laid her cheek against it, and felt comforted. He would come back, his things were still here.

A pair of gray flannel trousers was folded neatly across the metal bar fastened inside one door. She slipped them off the bar and held them up against herself, the belt at her own waistline. About six inches of the bottoms lay along the floor at her feet. He was tall. With a grateful smile at a spot in the air six inches above her head, she folded the trousers across the bar again, and closed the wardrobe.

As she did so, a long shiver ran through her, and uneasiness like a cold draught pervaded the room. For a moment, leaning against the edge of the wardrobe, she looked about her, puzzled. She had put back everything, exactly as she found it. She had touched nothing a maid with a duster might not have fingered—except perhaps his clothes. She had committed no sacrilege, surely. But something was wrong. She felt sick and weak, the way she had felt after influenza. And the room was—*different.*

"What's happened?" she whispered instinctively, as though the room could hear and answer. "What have I done?"

Rain was still falling outside, the gray windows were darkening, and the air was chill and dim. For the first time the room's silence was loud. Fright crept into her eyes—here, where she had always felt so safe and cherished. Something had gone out of the room, something friendly and protective, and in its place was emptiness, strangeness, and doubt.

She began to back towards the door, with wide, watchful eyes, as though the room might try to stop her. . . .

Alice was looking at her. The sphinxes were watching—smiling—waiting. The little brown pipe lay there beside them, *waiting.* Tobacco in the jar getting stale—his clothes, left hanging where moth could get at them—the letter to Thompson, never finished, never sent—what would Thompson think?—the calendar, static at June 5, 1936—two years to the day—but a man didn't just walk out for two years without packing his things—where had he gone?—where was he now?—what had taken him out of the room on the fifth of June and never let him come back?—how much longer would they all have to wait. . . .

When Aunt Effie came home from the sewing circle, she found Sabrina lying on her bed, and sent for the doctor. Sabrina lay very quietly, with her eyes wide open. Her lips were cold and bloodless. She would say nothing except that she didn't feel very well.

The doctor said it was a slight chill on the liver, and left some little white pills.

IV

MIST was creeping in over the Embankment from the River. Not an old-fashioned fog, for it was June in London. This was just a white blur, hanging still and muggy—a come-by-chance summer mist, local and ephemeral.

Big Ben had just struck ten P.M. when the policeman passed Cleopatra's Needle—which in fact has never had anything to do with Cleopatra—and glanced up as was his habit into the calm, bronze face of one of the attendant sphinxes. Same old thing, still there. It seemed to gaze beyond him, down river, waiting—but friendly in its very immobility on its low pedestal; dependable, changeless, receptive, content. The policeman liked the sphinxes. He liked to think of that quiet regard, unblinking and serene amid the noise and confusion on the night of the air raid in 1917 when a bomb struck nearby and flying fragments of steel scarred and pitted the base of the column. Mentally the policeman always saluted the sphinxes as he passed by on his rounds.

The Embankment was nearly clear of strollers tonight, in the freak mist, where from under one lamp post you could barely make out the glimmer of the next. In the policeman's wake, but unaware of him and unseen by him, a solitary young man moved aimlessly westward.

He was neatly dressed, with a white collar. It was only on a second glance that his genteel shabbiness became apparent. His soft brown hat was pulled low, and the remnant of a cigarette had burned to his fingertips. He dropped it listlessly on the pavement and as listlessly set his foot on it—a well-shaped, well-mended shoe. As he did so he became conscious of the still bronze face above him, veiled in mist, the eyes fixed down river, watching, waiting. . . .

For a moment the young man glared up at it, and it ignored him. Then he spoke to it aloud, but very low.

"All right, you!" he said to it, with half a lifetime of suppressed fury in the way the words came out between his teeth. "Go on, then—smile, damn you—*smile!*"

At once he glanced about him hastily to make sure no one had heard, and was glad of the muffling mist which pressed towards him from the River. He drifted up against the stone balustrade, and it was clammy to his hand. He peered over the edge. Mist hung between him and the water. It looked an endless drop. It looked attractive and peaceful and final. It looked so easy . . .

"Steady," said Hilary very quietly, emerging from the mist below the column. "None of that, my boy."

The young man glanced once behind him, and seemed to see an empty pavement. His eyes returned to where he knew the water must be. His left knee bent and began to move stealthily upward along the stone, his weight was shifting to his hands, which rested on the top. . . .

"It won't do, you know," said Hilary, standing there on the step beneath the column. "Come out of it."

"Here!" cried a voice from the mist to the left of them. "Here! Hi! I say!"

Sir Reginald Forsyth had lacked a cab to take him to the club in Piccadilly, after dining with a friend in the Temple. The port had been excellent. In fact, he had taken just that one last glass—. And then there weren't any cabs. Very well, he would walk, by Jove. No sort of walk at all, for a man in good condition, from the Temple to Piccadilly. To Sir Reginald, striding along the Embankment that evening with his top hat at the slightest angle and his white silk scarf floating free, even the mist was rosy. The Needle already, by Jove. He swung his stick in a gesture of greeting to the watching sphinxes. It was only then that he saw something which put him out of step with himself.

"Here! Hi! I say! You can't do that!" he cried, lunging forward with astounding agility for his age, weight, and state of repletion.

The slight, boyish figure was limp and docile in his grasp as he pulled it back off the stone balustrade.

"Now, then, what's it all about, eh?" Sir Reginald went on severely. "Trying to spoil my night's rest by committing suicide under my very nose! I call it abominable cheek, sir, and ruddy thoughtless of you, by Jove!"

"I should damn' well think so," said Hilary, half

sitting, half leaning now against the base of the column, watching them with amusement. He wore a plain dark suit and hat, and no topcoat, and had come to pay his respects to the sphinxes on his way to the club.

The salvaged young man reeled against the nearest pedestal and clung there, silent, his face hidden. Sir Reginald settled his own hat and regarded his catch aggressively.

"Well, what have you got to say for yourself?" he demanded. "Speak up!"

"You don't expect me to thank you, do you?" muttered the young man without moving.

"No—not yet. Only it would have been cold down there—and horrid wet, you know." Sir Reginald shivered graphically.

"What's that to you?"

"Shouldn't have slept a wink if I hadn't nabbed you in time!" The young man laughed at this, bitterly, and Sir Reginald took no notice of it. "What's your name?" he said.

"Does it matter?"

"Not a bit. What's your name?"

"John Chantrell."

"Well, Chantrell, what's the matter with you?" Sir Reginald laid a hand on the bony shoulder nearest him, and was shaken off. "Lost your job?" he inquired briskly.

"Job?" repeated the sullen voice. "Oh, no—if you can call it a job."

"Girl thrown you over?" suggested Sir Reginald, full of sympathy.

"There isn't a girl."

"What, no girl? Tck-tck!" Sir Reginald looked a little incredulous. He cast about in his mind, and tried again triumphantly. "Put your shirt on something that romped in last?"

"No."

"Well," said Sir Reginald, reaching for his note-case, "would a fiver see you through? 'Bout all I've got on me."

There was a long silence.

"No, thanks," said Chantrell, motionless against the pedestal.

"That's right." Sir Reginald tucked the thin folded paper into his protégé's coat pocket. "You have it. I've got another at home."

John Chantrell turned then, braced against the clammy stone, and spoke with biting scorn.

"You haul me down off the parapet—and offer me a five-pound note!" he said.

"Well, I—I—" Sir Reginald thrust a hasty hand into his trousers pocket in search of more.

"You won't miss it, will you!" John Chantrell accused him, through set teeth. "You've had a good dinner. You've got a soft bed waiting for you somewhere up West. You pay your tailor when you think of it, and your credit is good when you don't. You *smell* of money, and your club, and your claret, and your damned Corona-Coronas—"

With a murmur of apology, Sir Reginald fished out his cigar-case and proffered it. Chantrell waved it away rudely.

"I can't smoke cigars. They make me sick."

"Well, it beats me—" Sir Reginald meekly put away the cigar-case. "You've got a job, you haven't got a girl to treat you badly, and you don't need five pounds. And yet you try to jump in the River. It doesn't make sense."

At this point, Chantrell cracked up entirely. With a smothered sob he collapsed on the stone step beside the pedestal and buried his face in his hands. Sir Reginald stood regarding such indecent spiritual nakedness in some dismay. He found it difficult to believe that people behaved this way except on the films. All his social reflexes inclined him to apologize and back out, as though he had opened the wrong door.

"Stick to it, sir," Hilary encouraged him from beside the column at a little distance from them. "This wants handling."

Sir Reginald considered Chantrell solemnly a moment more, and then sat down beside him with a slight grunt on the lower step.

"Very well, let's philosophize together," he suggested. "Or would you rather go somewhere and have a drink? There's a little place over there in Villiers Street—"

"Please leave me alone," begged John Chantrell, and he meant it. "I'll be all right."

"Oh, no." Sir Reginald settled himself more firmly on the step. "Not now, I can't. The Orientals say that when you have saved a man's life it belongs henceforth to you. So I have the right to make a damn' nuisance of myself in your life for the rest of my days, and I intend to start now. 'Tisn't just morbid curiosity, my boy—whatever brought you to such a pass, and so forth—none of that. Though I must admit that at my age it seems a futile gesture voluntarily to leave this interesting world in search of a purely problematical peace." He paused. "Why did you want to do that, laddie?"

"I was all right," said John Chantrell sullenly, "until I suddenly looked up and caught *it*—smiling!" He gestured upward contemptuously at the sphinx above them.

"As though it knew all the answers." Hilary glanced up into the sphinx's face, and for a moment they seemed to look into each other's eyes, smiling the same small smile. "And it won't tell. And you're not allowed to look in the back of the book." The whole situation had a dream-like quality which was beginning to puzzle him. It was a queer homecoming—a queer sort of night altogether, with these two oddities perched absurdly on the step, absorbed in their argument, taking no more notice of him than if he had been invisible. Perhaps it was a dream, and he would wake up soon in his narrow bed in Peshawur. . . .

"Well, what if it does smile?" Sir Reginald was propounding reasonably. "What's the matter with that?"

"Please let me alone."

"I know. You don't want me doing you a bit of good. You've made up your mind you won't have it. But just you try and stop me. I've got all night."

"I said it had a right to smile!" John Chantrell returned a little hysterically to his grievance. "I said so to its face! What's it got to worry about? It's made of bronze! It doesn't have to eat—or sleep—or make a living! It doesn't even have to live!"

"Nor die," remarked Sir Reginald thoughtfully.

"Dying's easy enough!" cried Chantrell with his bitter laugh.

"That depends," said Hilary quietly where he stood, but Sir Reginald spoke simultaneously and so they did not hear.

"Jumping into the Thames is easy enough, you mean," Sir Reginald corrected him.

"Same thing," mumbled Chantrell.

"Not at all," objected Sir Reginald with a shudder. "Tell me, Chantrell—remember, I've got a Chinese right to know!—tell me exactly why you don't like it here."

"Oh, God—!" Chantrell lifted a haggard face from his hands to stare at his benefactor. "What is there to *like?* Ever since I can remember we've been sticking it—holding on—hoping—praying, I suppose—for what? You don't know anything about it, of course! You were young before the War. You had your cake! Let me ask *you* a question. What's the first thing you can remember?"

"First thing I can remember?" Sir Reginald knit his brows. "Let's see. You mean—"

"I mean 'way back," Chantrell interrupted passionately. "As far back as you can go. Fifty years, it might be. What's the first thing you can dig up?"

"Let me see, now," murmured Sir Reginald, playing the game with relish. " 'Way back as far as I can go, eh—good Lord, fifty years—you flatter me! Now let me see. I know! I've got it! I was taken to the theatre! *You* wouldn't know, though—it was *Iolanthe*. She was new then. How did it go—?" He broke off to hum a bar of the Westminster trio.

> " 'Never, never, never, never,
> Faint heart *nev*-er won fair la-dee—'

I always liked that bit. Seen it dozens of times since. But Gladstone was there that first night, I can remember their pointing him out to me. Grim old bird, Gladstone. But *you* wouldn't know about that," he concluded with mournful condescension.

"But I do know!" Chantrell contradicted him angrily. "I wasn't there, but I know exactly what you mean! Victoria was alive then. And little boys like you wore velvet suits with white collars. And there was pretty music and pretty laughter that was really gay! And the women's jewels were all real, and a man who could make fun of the Government in jolly rhymes was given a knighthood! Haven't I read about it all my life? *Of course* I know! But what about me? What about the first thing *I* can remember?"

"All right, now you tell one," agreed Sir Reginald promptly, playing the game.

"An air raid."

"Are you as young as *that?*" said Sir Reginald aghast.

"I'm as old as that. I was born to the War, *of* the War. I can't remember anything else. I can't remember my father very well, because I never saw much of him. I was the youngest of five. We were always a little hungry. We were always a little frightened. We were always brave, though—" He gave his bitter laugh. "—because Daddy was fighting for England, and that was a great honor! Well, finally he died for England—thrown away—wasted—futile—like all the rest of them!" He buried his face in his hands again.

"Wasted?" repeated Hilary, who was listening intently.

"I don't pretend to mourn my father as an individual," admitted Chantrell from behind his shielding hands. "It isn't that. He was nothing to me, personally. I cried because the others did. *They* missed him. He was a jolly man, they tell me, who used to come home with a bag of boiled sweets in his pocket. Well, what was the good of his dying, like that? What's the good of anything? What's England worth—now?"

"England's the sanest spot on the earth today," maintained Sir Reginald stoutly.

"I don't know about sane," said Chantrell, "but I

wouldn't give tuppence for England today, freehold. Not but what I do pay the Government considerably more than that each year for the privilege of being alive in England!"

"Exactly," said Hilary. "And worth it too."

"That's the point," said Sir Reginald. "It *is* a privilege, these days."

"And *your* income tax," pursued Chantrell, glaring at him, "is probably a good deal more than I can earn in a year."

"I don't doubt it," agreed Sir Reginald pacifically.

"Well, don't you *care?* Don't you ever wish you could hang on to all that money for yourself? Or have you got so much it doesn't matter?"

"Of course it matters," Sir Reginald admitted cheerfully. "Matters like hell, sometimes. But as I look round the world today, I can't say I grudge it to 'em. To the fellas that run the country, I mean. As I look round, I feel England's got something to show for my money, and yours, and the next man's."

"And when you die," Chantrell reminded him, "they'll build another battleship out of the proceeds."

"That might be a good idea too," nodded Sir Reginald.

"More guns—more ships—more bombers!" cried Chantrell with sarcasm. "More gas-masks—more shells—more tanks! *Why?* So it can all happen again! So I can go out and get killed like my father, but before I can try to make some woman happy, before I've seen a son—"

"Maybe not," Sir Reginald told him gently. "Maybe we'll pull through. Mind you, I'm no optimist. I don't like the looks of things any better than you do. But look round a bit. Tell me some other city in Europe you'd rather be in tonight, sitting on a damp stone step under a statue cursing out the Government to a total stranger. See what I mean?"

There was a silence.

"Show us a better 'ole, old boy," suggested Hilary softly.

Sir Reginald appeared to consider this, gazing into the middle distance.

"Ever been abroad?" he queried.

"Abroad! Me?" Chantrell's lip curled. "That's a fairly funny question!"

"You ought to go clean round the world," Sir Reginald told him. "Don't miss out anything. Berlin—Paris—Prague—Vienna—Rome—oh, yes, and Leningrad and Moscow—Palestine—India—don't forget China and Japan—Mexico—Chicago—'tisn't so bad in Chicago as it used to be—New York—nice spot of election coming on there pretty soon—they have enough to eat, though. Well, so have we. I think, take it all in all, and one thing with another, you'd be willing to come back home."

"Home to what?" Chantrell spread his bony, well-kept hands. "A furnished room in Kilburn—a stool in a long row of stools, and endless columns of marching figures—pounds, shillings, and pence belonging to somebody else—somebody like you!"

"You mean you're one of those fellows in a bank?" Sir Reginald's tone became deeply sympathetic.

"Tea and an egg for lunch," Chantrell went on, relentlessly. "Shepherd's pie for dinner. Always the cheapest thing on the menu, and no coffee because it's extra. Always the cheapest seat at the cinema, and always a cinema because it's cheaper than the theatre. Second-hand books, and go without cigarettes to buy them—"

"Do you like to read?" interrupted Sir Reginald in some surprise. "Got rather a good library myself. Care to use it?"

"How do you know I won't pinch the silver candlesticks when I go?" inquired Chantrell with flimsy cynicism.

"Wouldn't be much good to you, would they?" Sir Reginald grinned at him amiably.

"No, and neither will your library, thank you very much! I'm past caring now. What's the good? I get down off that stool at night with my brains addled and useless. I go and stuff myself with dull cheap food because I'm empty. I let the girls alone because I can't afford to fall decently in love and I don't care about the other thing. I exist. And the next day it's all to do over again. And it must go on—it must! I can't stop. I daren't think of losing my job. I must hang on and on, because if I let go I starve. So what does it all come to?" He thrust his hand into his coat pocket and brought out the fiver. "Here. I don't need this."

Sir Reginald laid his card on top of the note and forced both back into Chantrell's hand.

"Come and see me," he said.

"Thanks, I'd rather not."

"Next time," said Sir Reginald with his cheerful disregard of opposition, "you come and dine with me." He rose, boosting himself off the low step by a heavy hand on Chantrell's shoulder.

"In these clothes?" suggested Chantrell ironically.

"Why not? Just the two of us. No females in my household, except the cook. It'd be a change, don't you think—for both of us. Y'know, I get fed up too, in my way. Getting to the age where the same old friends are thinning out. Got to make new ones." His smile was kindly and free of patronage, even a bit wistful. "How about it?"

"You're very good, sir," said Chantrell, with a sudden return to his habitual listless courtesy.

"Maybe. Maybe not. Do what I can." He contemplated Chantrell a moment more, standing over the slack young body on the step. Chantrell was leaning back against the pedestal, his face hidden by the brim of his hat, drowsy with nervous exhaustion. "That's better," Sir Reginald said, perceiving that the immediate crisis was over. "You wouldn't like to give me your word of honor you won't go fooling about with the River again?"

"No," said Chantrell deliberately, without looking at him. "I wouldn't like to."

"Suppose we just leave it that you'll come and see me first," persisted Sir Reginald.

Chantrell did not reply.

"It's no good trying to dodge things, y'know. You must just serve your time here like the rest of us," Sir Reginald explained patiently, and groped for words to clothe thoughts he had never attempted to utter before. "There's some sort of pattern," he brought out finally. "If you muck it up you lose your last chance."

"How did you know that?" said Hilary.

"Maybe you think because I'm too well fed I've missed out the way you feel tonight," Sir Reginald continued, contemplating the motionless figure slumped against the pedestal. "You're wrong, boy. I've seen lots of nights when tomorrow wasn't worth waiting for. That was a long time ago. But I haven't forgotten. It won't do, though. You'll see that one day."

He paused. Chantrell kept his head down, and said nothing—apparently was not even listening any more.

"Well—that's that," said Sir Reginald, feeling a little flat.

"Tell him the rest of it," Hilary said quickly. "Tell him how you know."

Sir Reginald lingered, his big shoulders rather bowed, his shadow a formless blob beside him in the feeble light from the street lamp.

"I suppose I may as well tell you how I'm so sure about it," he said slowly. " 'Tisn't a thing I speak of generally. I'd like to think I wasn't wasting it—now."

"Some of it will sink in, sir," said Hilary.

"Once I loved a woman who seemed to me so perfect that there weren't any other women in the world," said Sir Reginald. "She married another fellow—she wasn't happy with him—and then she died. I nearly went crazy. I thought of all the short cuts I could take to follow her. I went into the subject pretty thoroughly at the time. But that's against the rules. And if you break the rules, you won't come out even. The thing you're reaching for won't be there till it's time for you to have it. You must live out your way to it the best you can, with whatever tools you can lay your hands on. So I go to the club, and I chivvy my pals, and I enjoy my food—and now and then I get a bit boozy—it all helps. See what I mean?"

"You've put it better than I could have done," said Hilary.

"I need a drink," said Sir Reginald abruptly, pulling himself together with a shrug of his massive shoulders. "Been talking too much. Don't usually tell the story of my life. Queer sort of weather, anyway. Gets in your bones." He decided tactfully to let it go at that. "Good-night, laddie," he said, and walked on briskly into the white mist, towards that place in Villiers Street.

Hilary, from the base of the column, watched him go. Then he moved forward slowly and took Sir Reginald's seat on the step beside Chantrell, who still ignored his presence and did not stir.

"Nobody asked me," said Hilary, "but the first thing

I can remember is a tea-table on the lawn, with flecks of sunlight glinting on the silver, and men in white coming back from tennis. I did know my father quite well. He was killed in Palestine in 1917. Wasted, I believe you said. But I know one thing. He wouldn't think so." He waited. John Chantrell sat in sullen silence. "I would like to say just this, if you don't mind. You're fed to the back teeth, I know, with things the way they are. And you wouldn't like my sort of life any better than the one you've got, though it happens to suit me down to the ground. My father wasn't just a soldier. He had a gift of languages and he used to do special jobs on the side. He didn't want me to be a soldier either. He said any blundering fool could always die for his country. He said that sort of thing would go out of fashion when the War ended. Perhaps he was wrong. Anyway, I've tried to carry on from where he left off. I work alone a lot, with plenty of time to think. I've been away from England quite a while, out East. You might call it sentimentalizing—but I've seen the time when I wanted England, and what England stands for, more than I wanted immortality. Maybe England's gone all to pot while my back was turned—but on the other hand, I assure you it looks like heaven to me!"

The lax figure beside him maintained its obstinate silence. He leaned forward to peer under the defensive hat brim. Drugged by exhaustion and emotional relief, John Chantrell drowsed against the cold stone. Hilary had a sudden impulse to shake him awake again, march him off for a drink, and shove him on a bus for Kilburn. But he dismissed it, feeling shy and futile and uncertain. He rose, and stood looking up at the great bronze face above them.

"Do you think, if I'm very careful not to jar myself or knock into anything, I can get as far as the club and have a drink there before I wake up?" he inquired of it, and there was naturally no reply. "I'm going to try, anyway. I'd like to see London again, even if it's only a dream. I'll leave this to you," he told the sphinx, with a glance at Chantrell, and turned away westward, into the mist.

The old boy was quite right, and he had put things very well indeed. There was some sort of schedule somewhere, some sort of Olympian Bradshaw, and you caught the trains as they came along. You mustn't let one go by, and you mustn't try for the one in front. That was cheating. You couldn't cheat successfully with the Olympians, they dealt the cards and they held all the aces. . . .

I'm mixing my metaphors, Hilary thought, as he turned into Northumberland Avenue and caught sight of Nelson on his column. No mist in Trafalgar Square. That was queer. London was suddenly in sharper focus as he reached Cockspur Street and heard taxi horns and passed a policeman with a short rolled mackintosh hooked to his belt in a normal sort of way, and noticed that the pavement was up in the Haymarket as usual.

But it was still rather like a dream, to sight the Carlton again, with Pall Mall just ahead. . . . Maybe I never really saw those two blokes at all, he thought, crossing Waterloo Place. Maybe I was talking to myself. It *is* a queer night, I'll have a stiff one at the club. . . .

V

HILARY SHENSTONE and his brother George, dissimilar in appearance and temperament as two brothers can be, had the same favorite club in Pall Mall, though each preferred it for a different reason. George went there because it was most convenient to his West End orbit, and because its wines and cigars were superior. Hilary frequented it, when he was in London, because various pals of his father's could still be found there, and because to a man returned from heathen lands its upholstered silences epitomized to the greatest degree the luxuries of English civilization.

The usual after-dinner peace brooded over its lounge that June evening. Semi-recumbent, contented figures were sunk behind newspapers in armchairs. The air was fragrant with pipe smoke and good cigars. An occasional glass stood half empty on a smoking-table. The high beamed ceiling, the spacious walls, absorbed the murmur of low voices here and there.

In a big chair by the fireplace George Shenstone was smoking a cigar and working his way without a smile through the newest *Punch*. He was fair, and a little thick through the neck, and still young enough to enjoy being sardonic. Near him old Calthorpe—he was barely fifty, and old was a term of affection—sat behind the *Standard*, ruddy and cheerful, wise in the ways of men and of horses. On the other side of a table full of periodicals Lord Totleigh, father of the Honorable Alice, had his nose in the *Illustrated London News*, and was not pleased with what he saw there. He was a gentle, tired, humorous man with a white mustache.

"Chamberlain has been very clever, if you ask me," said Calthorpe to the world in general. "Damned clever bird he is!"

"What, again?" said George lazily.

"What's he up to now?" Totleigh queried with friendly skepticism. "More Anglo-Italian agreement?"

"He'll never bring it off," said George, turning a page. "Never in this world. Anyway, Spain is too far gone."

The exact gist of this was not clear to them, so they left it.

"It's not Spain, but Czechoslovakia, that will stretch him," Calthorpe admitted. "I don't like it. It's everybody's fault, including Czechoslovakia's. I don't like it."

"It'll get worse and worse," said George, without looking up from *Punch*, "and finally somebody over there will go *bang!* and then we'll all be for it."

Calthorpe and Totleigh exchanged entirely expressionless glances, and there was silence while each returned to his paper. After several minutes of this Totleigh gave a despairing grunt and flung out the *News* at them, open.

"Look at that!" he commanded them. "India's a mess.

It's always been a mess, and I'm afraid it always will be!"

Calthorpe glanced briefly at the paper. Waziristan again.

"Is Hilary still out there?" he inquired of George.

"Oh, yes, so far as anybody knows," said Hilary's brother, grinding his teeth on a yawn. "His leave is overdue, but Hilary never writes."

"What's he doing out there now?"

"Sh!" said George. "Not so loud. Hilary moves in a cloud these days. One of those hush-hush expeditions up north."

"Oh, I say, have they given him another one of those nasty Border jobs?" said Calthorpe in genuine concern.

"Don't feel sorry for him, he loves it," objected Hilary's brother. "Keep the flag flyin'—that sort of thing! Hilary's exactly like father, and father might have been something that Kipling wrote."

"I liked your father, George," Calthorpe reminded him gently.

"So did I," George assured him unemotionally. "But it was right that he shouldn't survive the War. He'd be an uncomfortable anachronism. Hilary is."

"I've got an idea, George," said Totleigh, moving round to the hearthrug and taking a stance there while he filled his pipe, "I've got an idea, George, that what this world needs is more anachronisms!"

"Perhaps you're right," George conceded sweetly. "Perhaps Hilary's right too. Mother's getting a bit anxious about him, but I tell her we've had scares before."

"Alice is worrying, I think," said her father. "I must say, Hilary might let her hear a little oftener."

"What you want is for Hilary to come back and marry the gel and start raising a crop of little anachronisms," accused Calthorpe, measuring off with his hand several steps a few feet from the ground absurdly. "Let the boy alone. Would to God we had more like him! Their fathers were all killed off in the War, and the young ones were shoved into shoes too big for them too soon. But Hilary knows what he's about. You can't tie his sort by the leg, and we need 'em where they are. Let the girls wait, it's worth it!"

"Imperialist!" remarked Totleigh in affectionate reproof.

"I can think of worse names," said Calthorpe cheerfully, "and better men to call by it!"

"What *did* Gladstone say in '84?" inquired George ironically.

"If you live long enough," Calthorpe told him with studied kindness, "you'll be able to see, as we do, that England as an institution had been in almost continuous danger of collapse or extinction ever since the Wars of the Roses—and that its anachronisms, if we agree to call them that, are an important part of its survival."

"I suppose so," George agreed heavily. "I suppose you're all perfectly right. I suppose one should give thanks fasting even for death and taxes!"

"Oh, taxes!" murmured Totleigh on the hearthrug. "You've got a tenant for Nuns Farthing, what are *you* grousing about? I've got four houses on my hands and can't let one of 'em!"

"You've let Nuns Farthing, George?" exclaimed Calthorpe in surprise.

"Yes, and that's a piece of luck if you like! Wish he'd buy instead of letting. Rum old blighter out of the British Museum. Writes about prehistoric barrows and old British thingummies. Wanted to go and live near Dolebury Camp. Got a couple of unfortunate female belongings, sister and a kid. Must be nice for them!"

"I used to go down there quite a lot before the War," mused Calthorpe. "You and Hilary and Alice were children. Used to have tea under a big tree on the lawn—" He pulled himself out of reverie with a long sigh. "Ah, well, something like those days will come again, please God! Don't you sell the place, George. You hang on to it for your old age!"

"Yes, and pay taxes on it meanwhile!" growled George. "But try and get mother to live there! Or Alice either, for that matter!" He rose, with an ill-smothered yawn. "Hilary can have it," he said, "for *his* old age! Good-night, sir."

They waited in noncommittal silence till he was quite gone. Then they looked at each other, and old Lord Totleigh's quizzical brows went still higher.

"He's right about Alice, anyway," he admitted. "She doesn't like living in the country."

"How does she feel about living in Waziristan?" queried Calthorpe drily. "Or is that all off?"

"I don't know—I give up—I can't keep track of things," Alice's father confessed fretfully. "At one time there was a sort of understanding, I believe it's called, between Alice and Hilary, as you know. They're second cousins—more or less grew up together. But now—I don't know—he's been away two years. She seems to be seeing quite a lot of George lately, if it comes to that."

Because of his own guilty preference for Hilary, Calthorpe kept his eyes on the floor and forbore to remark that George seemed rather more Alice's sort. Totleigh nearly said it for him.

"Of course George was a lot older when they were kids. Now the difference in their ages doesn't matter so much. Or does it? Of course I'd rather it was Hilary. But on the other hand—" He petered out, for he too was aware that George, with his very decent income and settled habits, was surely more Alice's sort. "I give up," he said again helplessly. "You can't run other people's lives for them."

At that moment Denby of the Home Office entered the room, glanced round quickly, and made for Totleigh on the hearthrug. Hilary arrived on the threshold just behind him and paused there, watching Denby cross the room.

The feeling that he must wake up any moment now had been growing stronger as he approached the club, while the reality of London wavered and receded. Then things began to go askew, as they always do in even the most vivid dreams—discrepancies—omissions—and a looming sense of something dreadfully wrong. First, he discovered he couldn't remember anything about the voyage home. And then it was a new commissionaire at the club door, in place of old Simpson, who must have died at last. The new man naturally hadn't recognized him, and the two members who had passed through the swing door just ahead of him were strangers to Hilary. It was not quite the entrance he had counted on. The commissionaire greeted the other two and turned away to find a telephone message. None of them took any notice of Hilary, so he tossed his hat onto a peg and started towards the lounge.

Denby was crossing the hall from the writing-room a few yards away, and Hilary cried his name with relief. But Denby went on, not hearing, into the lounge. Hilary followed, with an idea of moving very carefully now, so as not to jar himself awake. He paused on the threshold. Old Calthorpe was there, and Alice's father stood on the hearthrug with his pipe. . . .

"—I give up—you can't run other people's lives for them—"

They saw Denby then, and welcomed him. None of them glanced towards the door where Hilary stood. He drew a few steps nearer, cautiously. He must hear, before he woke. Someone brushed past him on the way out. . . .

"You look as though you'd had a bit of a jolt," said Calthorpe to Denby.

"We're full of jolts at the Home Office," replied Denby, and Hilary saw that he looked old and tired. "But this one pretty well floors me."

"Bad news from somewhere?" Totleigh suggested sympathetically.

"From India—as usual. Hilary Shenstone is dead. One job too many up beyond Peshawur. Nobody's fault, I suppose—"

Poor old Denby, Hilary was thinking. This has hit him hard. Poor old— *What?* Dead. *Who?*

"But his brother George was sitting here just now—" began Calthorpe, dazed.

"He doesn't know yet. The family will be notified tomorrow. One or two things have to be dealt with first. I shouldn't have mentioned it, but—I loved his father."

The family will be notified. . . . A familiar Home Office phrase, as Hilary well knew. This wouldn't do, he was ready to wake up now, this was nightmare. They were talking about him. It was his father Denby had loved, his family which would be . . . Oh, yes, most decidedly, it was time to wake up now. . . .

"It's always the wrong one," Denby was saying. "All through the War, it seemed to be always the wrong one, the *best* one, first. Maybe there's some reason in it, I don't know— But I'm going to blame Pearson for this, at least till I know differently. He should have sent more men, instead of Bill Dalton alone. He should have sent sooner—"

Pearson. Yes, of course . . . there was a job to do for

Pearson. . . . *You'll have to write my family, Bill.* . . . He'd said that himself . . . after the crash. . . .

"Hilary was dead of a gunshot wound when the rescue plane arrived," Denby was saying. "Nothing could have saved him, once he was hit, but—I blame Pearson."

Dead. He remembered now. . . . Dalton sitting beside him, under the wing of the useless plane. . . . His side was hurting . . . and he must get back to England . . . why? . . . something he had to do . . . what was the date? . . . the nuns would know how to say it. . . . *Oh, God, let me have England instead.* . . . He had prayed. . . . They had heard him. . . . Somewhere, somebody had heard him. . . . But this wasn't England. . . . It was Eternity. . . .

VI

HE stood there in the warm, familiar surroundings of his club in Pall Mall and knew that he was dead. But on the Embankment just now—yes, of course—they hadn't spoken to him, had they—they hadn't once looked his way—*because they hadn't known he was there.*

Dead. He realized it with a terror he had never known on earth, a helpless, unreasoning panic which fluttered and struggled and strained like the wings of a frantic bird. The commissionaire in the hall—the men who went through the door just ahead of him—Denby crossing the marble floor towards the lounge—none of them had known he was there. They couldn't see him. They couldn't hear him. He was cut off from them forever—disembodied—invisible—exiled. *Dead.*

Slowly, in surroundings so entirely sane, his own scattered sanity reasserted itself. Slowly he emerged from terror and looked about him, taking stock. He had come back. He had longed to come, and here he was. Why? Was a dying man's prayer always answered? Could a man in his last moments make his own hereafter? And while he stood there among them, feeling quite himself, not dreaming after all, he heard them saying that he had been buried at Peshawur.

Slowly the freakish humor of it began to reach him. Somebody, somewhere, had done it on him. He had asked, and it had been given. Was there laughter in heaven? No. No, this could not really be. It was some form of delusion still—fever—nightmare—delirium. . . . He would prove to himself now, at once, that this thing simply hadn't happened. He would speak to Denby—and then they would turn to him with incredulous looks, seize his hands, order drinks all round. Or else he would wake in a cold sweat in that narrow white room in Peshawur. Or else . . .

"*What about Dalton?*" he demanded, approaching the group round the hearth. "*Did they get Dalton back safe?*"

"Dalton's report is coming by air mail," said Denby. "He's had rather a bad time. No water where they crashed. But he'll pull through."

There, you see? It worked. Denby had heard and answered his question. But no one was looking at him. Must try again. Must prove . . .

"*Did Dalton write my family too?*" he asked, and laid his hand on Denby's shoulder.

He knew then. He had the answer. Denby was shaken by a long shiver, and put a hand to his head.

"Damn," said Denby apologetically. "I—I need a drink, somebody."

"Have my brandy, old boy." Calthorpe thrust a full

glass into Denby's hand and rang the bell. "Steady, now —let's sit down. We all need a stiff one, I'm thinking."

That's funny, thought Hilary. No drink for me.

Looking from one to another of their grave, lined faces, he suddenly abandoned all hope for himself. Too many times he had made one in a stricken circle like this. Too many drinks had been ordered by himself in similar circumstances for him to ignore the signs. Stirrup cups, you called them in Lahore. He was dead, all right. Denby didn't make mistakes. Denby had the facts. He began to feel a little embarrassed, like an inadvertent eavesdropper. It was indecent to attend his own wake. He supposed he ought to go. Where?

"I say, Totleigh—" Denby raised his head from the glass. "Bit of a blow for your girl, too—Alice, I mean— I mean, weren't they—"

"Presumably they were," said Totleigh moodily, his tall thin figure drooping against the mantelpiece. "One never knows these days what one's young people are really about, does one? She's been seeing quite a lot of his brother lately. It will be hard on her, of course, in any case, but—I don't know—"

Hilary was staring at him. George and Alice? For a moment there was no reaction, and he wondered if he had conveniently left his emotions somewhere along the way. Of course Alice had always hated his job—even tried to make him promise to give it up and stay in England. It was because he had half expected this to be his last undertaking before handing in his resignation that he had been so prompt and willing on the day that the Home Office had rung through to Nuns Farthing. So George was cutting in, was he. One must look into this.

"I'm thinking Alice won't miss him as much as we do, at that," said Totleigh, and glanced round at them piteously from the hearthrug. "I always thought of him almost as a son. I've never felt that way about George, somehow— Three double brandies," he added, as a club servant appeared in answer to the bell.

But this is awful, thought Hilary. They'll have me crying over them in a minute. It's not as bad as all that, chaps, really it isn't, he wanted to say. . . .

"If it's any satisfaction to us," Denby was saying to the rest of them, "he had finished the job before they got him. The mullah is caught red-handed. If that's any comfort," he muttered, contemplating the amber liquid in his glass. "And I suppose it ought to be."

"It ought to be to Hilary," said Calthorpe grimly.

And it was, but Hilary had had enough of this. He couldn't go on standing there and watch them break their hearts over him. He must take himself off till they came round a bit. The brandies would fix them up. . . . He turned away aimlessly, and sidestepped the man returning with a tray on which sat three tall glasses and a siphon.

No drink for Hilary, he thought. And I ought to need it worse than they do.

Calthorpe's quiet voice reached him again on the threshold.

"One for the road," said Calthorpe, as he lifted his glass.

Hilary drifted out into the entrance hall and collected his hat from the peg. The commissionaire was writing nearsightedly in the message book and did not raise his eyes.

Well, what next? What was the good of it, like this? How did one pass one's time? *Time?* There was no such thing as time, any more, for him. . . .

Lost in loneliness, and feeling very strange, Hilary pushed open the swing door and went out onto the step. From there he glanced back idly. The commissionaire was gaping at the door, which still swung slightly from Hilary's passage. The hall was empty. No one had gone in or out. The commissionaire was seeing things.

Hilary watched him, grinning, from the step. The situation suddenly began to have possibilities. One could amuse oneself, after all. Why not endow the club with a mystery? What if word went round tomorrow that Hilary Shenstone had occupied his old room the night after he was buried out in Peshawur—slept in his bed, ran his bath water—left no luggage. It would make history in Pall Mall. Only they'd never let it go beyond the four walls of the club. They wouldn't dare, because they'd be laughed at by all the other clubs.

The idea of spending the night in his usual bedroom in the club appealed to him. At least it would be cozier than the doorstep, and tomorrow morning he would look in on his mother in Park Street. Yes, and George. Fancy George setting his cap at Alice. . . .

But with his hand on the swing door again, he hesitated. He couldn't push it. Not again, with the commissionaire still there. Feeling self-conscious and silly, he hung about on the step outside, waiting for someone to open the door for him. It was late. No one was likely to be coming in from the street. Some of them inside would be going home presently. There was no hurry. There would never be any hurry again. . . .

At last a young man in an opera hat did come out—another new member. He gave the door a vigorous push and Hilary was able to step through on its second swing. In the hall again he skipped up the stairs to the bedroom floor and went along the passage to his right, turned the knob of the door to the room he always occupied, and opened the door briskly.

The light was on, and a fat little man in a pince-nez was sitting up in bed reading.

"*Oh, sorry*—" said Hilary, halting in his tracks.

The fat little man was staring through him at the open door. It was fairly obvious that he saw and heard nothing to account for it. He looked ready to scream.

Hilary considered. Would it be more tactful to close the door again, or leave it as it was? He backed out uncertainly into the passage. The little man pulled himself together with an effort, got out of bed and slammed the door to. He wore a nightshirt.

Hilary stole away down the passage, guiltily. One

must be more careful. One mustn't go barging in and out of places like this. At the same time, it would be nice to find a vacant room to spend the night in.

A line of light under the next door on the right showed that that room too was occupied. A peek through the keyhole of the one beyond proved the same.

At last he came to a room that was dark. Cautiously now he turned the knob and with a glance over his shoulder at the empty passage peered round the edge of the door. Light from a street-lamp outside showed the curtains undrawn and the bed not turned down. He nipped inside and shot the bolt on himself.

It was all very embarrassing.

VII

THE morning was sunny and warm. For a long time he stood at the window which faced towards the treetops in the Mall. Breakfast? Apparently he had no need for breakfast, and he knew a passing regret for the lost flavor of bacon and coffee, and the deep satisfaction of the first pipe of the day. Odd, the things that were left to him and the things that were taken away. He had a desire to look at flower-beds and green lawns, and get himself sorted out. There would be roses in bloom over beyond the Achilles, and perhaps delphiniums. One could always get a lot of thinking done along the side of the Serpentine. . . .

The truth was, he felt timid about going out into broad daylight. He told himself grimly that he could not stay locked up in a room at the club for the rest of time. No one had seen him last night. No one would see him now. But it would be only tactful to manage so that no one got unnecessary shocks. The thing was to get out while it was still early. In the Park it wouldn't matter. He could walk on the grass and look at the flowers.

He unbolted the door and listened—slipped out into the deserted passage, pulling the door shut behind him.

Coming stealthily round the corner to the stairhead, he brought up short at sight of an old club servant who knelt in the middle of the steps doing the brass rods and whistling softly through his teeth. Well, here goes. Hilary brushed past, against the paneling on the wall side. The servant was unaware. Hilary went more boldly down into the hall and took up a position near the door. He saw the advantages of not needing breakfast. Robbing the kitchen would have presented difficulties.

The day porter, a familiar face again, came obligingly and set the two swing-doors wide open to the morning air, kicking a wooden wedge under each. Hilary walked out onto the step and surveyed London. Just the same and ever changing. Good old London.

For several hours, tireless, invisible, feasting his sight, he roamed the streets and parks of the West End. He stood beside the Serpentine and watched the ducks being fed from paper bags, and the little old man beloved of the pigeons. He inspected minutely the state of the flower-beds, and watched dispassionately several broad-beamed young women bouncing healthfully along Rotten Row. If a woman could see herself, mounted, from behind, wearing breeches . . . Oh, well, sidesaddle was bad for the unborn generation to come.

The morning passed, and it wasn't so bad. Apparently one would get used to this sort of thing. He wondered how many more of his kind there were in the streets of London, and if they could see each other, and recognize a fellow drifter between the worlds. Everyone looked quite normal. Perhaps he was the only one who haunted London that day.

Every now and then he confronted the matter of George and Alice, with a growing curiosity. Of course as soon as they learned what had happened to him they would be free. . . . He wondered how they would take it, and knew that he meant to go and see. It wasn't decent to watch and listen to them today, of course, except that they would never know. But through them he might find the key to this fantastic adventure of his.

Again and again the dim presentiment passed through him of something awaiting him somewhere which would explain everything. He had not finished yet. He was here for some purpose which was still formless and beyond his reach. He was here to find something, to learn something, to see or hear something which still eluded him. When he got to it he would know the reason for the extraordinary thing which was happening to him. By some freak of time and space he was permitted to seek his destiny even after death should have solved it. But as yet he lacked all guidance, awaiting some message which seemed not to come through.

Towards lunch time he mounted the steps of his mother's little house in Park Street. It was George's green Rolls-Bentley four-seater, he supposed, which stood at the curb. A noisy brute of a car, and just what George would drive. Automatically he searched his pockets—damn—no keys—Dalton had his keys, in Peshawur. He eyed the solid door thoughtfully. Locked, of course. If one rang, Hinton the parlormaid would open it. . . .

Round the corner came two quite correct little boys, brothers, dressed alike in gray suits wth bare knees and white collars. With them was a lively spaniel, off his lead, which dangled from the younger boy's hand. Eminently well-behaved, they came level with the bottom of the steps where he stood—they were moving briskly, absorbed in the dog. Hilary pressed the bell.

The little boys broke into a brief run in an effort to refasten the lead to the frisky dog's collar. They were still chasing him busily, several houses further down the street when Hinton opened the door to an empty doormat. Hilary slipped past her into the hall. With a dark look after the innocent pair with the spaniel, Hinton shut the door smartly and returned to the kitchen, muttering.

Hilary mounted the familiar carpeted stairs to his mother's sitting-room, feeling again the awkwardness of all this eavesdropping, but driven by his earnest need of an answer to the riddle of his own situation.

He heard voices, and the door stood open.

"Cocktails, mater," George was saying decisively. "Too much sherry lately—makes me liverish."

"Oh? Well, ring the bell, dear, and just tell Hinton what you want," their mother's light, cheerful voice advised him. "Alice said one-fifteen for lunch. She's at the hairdresser's till one."

Not even George's liver could depress Mrs. Shenstone's naturally gay and inconsequential spirit. She was one of that unique race of Englishwomen who lived through four years of the Great War without breaking down; and she was of the species which for the last twenty years has gone on being bright and competent and sane by the simple expedient of never once coming into focus. A pleasant, busy vagueness is their salvation. They exist in a happy haze of trivialities. It is a sort of nirvana. They earned it.

Hilary paused on the threshold and stood looking into the sunny room, and feeling bitterly sorry for himself. Everything was so entirely as usual here. Alice was expected to lunch—cocktails would come up on a clinking tray—his mother was at her writing-table in a becoming gown someone ought to praise—old George with his finger on the bell and his eye on the lunch-time racing-form. . . .

Home again. But nobody looking up to say, "Hello, dear, what's the news?" in the vague, charming way his mother always did whenever anyone came in that door. . . .

Obviously they didn't know yet, about him. The Home Office was taking its time. Here they were, all having lunch together, and any minute a telegram would come through from the Home Office . . .

"I say, there's a damned silly story going round the club," said George. "Ponsonby swears he had a ghost in his room last night."

"At the *club?*" Their mother looked up from her letter-writing with a skeptical smile.

"Yes, at the club!" George affirmed, and grinned.

"*It was me*," said Hilary tentatively, half expecting, half hoping they would hear, and turn on him with incredulous hoots of rude family laughter. But—

"Nonsense, he'd been drinking," she cried, her incredulity all for Ponsonby.

"Ponsonby's a teetotaler," said George.

"Then no wonder he sees things!" she concluded logically. "What happened, to make him think it was a ghost?"

"Well, Ponsonby says he was in bed reading, when the door suddenly swung open as though someone had turned the knob from the passage."

"Yes—and hadn't someone?"

"Not a soul. There was nobody there. That is, nobody he could *see*. He was frightfully upset!"

"*I said I was sorry*," said Hilary in his own defense.

"Men's clubs are full of practical jokers," asserted their mother.

"Ah, but Ponsonby swears he pulled himself together at once and jumped out of bed to close the door. The passage was empty. But he's positive that Something had opened that door and was surprised to see him there, and went away, leaving it open."

"*He'd have felt worse if I'd closed it again*," insisted Hilary.

"I never heard of anything so absurd!" she cried. "The latch gave in a draught, of course."

"I know. We all said that. But there's another thing."

"Well, what?"

"Last night somebody slept in a room that was supposed to be empty."

"Oh, George, really!"

"I'm only telling you what they said! A room that hadn't been booked for several nights had its bed slept in last night. But there's no trace of the occupant.—Hinton, if you'll bring up the makings," added George, "I'll shake up a White Lady before lunch."

"Yes, sir," said Hinton, and withdrew again.

"And that's not all," George continued impressively, and produced the ultimate manifestation. "The fellow in the next room heard the bath water being run by the fellow in the empty room."

"Now, George, you're not trying to tell me their ghost took a bath!"

"That's the story! Ponsonby is going to write to the Society for Psychical Research, so you see how well it's gone with him!"

"Men are so silly! He was probably scaring himself to death with a detective story when it happened. I can always believe the house is full of burglars or things that knock on tables if I read Dorothy Sayers in bed. George, I've had another letter from those people down at Nuns Farthing."

"*What people?*" demanded Hilary, astonished.

"The Archers again?" George sighed with resignation. "Well, what do they want now?"

"It's that fussy woman, she writes all the letters, I'm sure Professor Archer wouldn't know or care if the roof blew off. Anyway, the kitchen flue has got to be cleaned out, and she thinks perhaps all the chimneys ought to be swept at the same time, and besides that they want that tree down at the end of the drive where it joins the road. They say it's dangerous—in the way, you know."

"That tree has been there a good many years and nobody has run afoul of it yet," said George, a bit pompously. "Not even in the old days of coaches. It must have been quite a trick to get a coach and four round it and into the road going east, but any modern conveyance can do it on two wheels."

"Well, apparently the butcher's boy did smash himself up, on his bicycle. There was a car coming from the left, and in avoiding it the boy hit the tree and broke his collar-bone."

"Silly fool, he must have been going hell-for-leather at the turn."

"Perhaps if we put up a nice little sign, not too large a one, of course, saying 'Concealed Drive'—"

"I've done that already. They're a damned nuisance, those people, I almost wish we'd never let the place!"

"*Let Nuns Farthing!*" cried Hilary in surprise. "*You might have mentioned it to me!*"

"If they'd only buy it—" she began, and hesitated.

"You can't sell a place like that nowadays, mater, the market is stiff with them. It's too big and too far from Town—and too expensive to keep up!"

"Your father was fond of it," she sighed. "Hilary likes it too, when he's at home."

"Then let Hilary stay at home and look after it!" growled George. "Just because I'm the elder I'm stuck with it! Does he expect me to keep the place going forever just for him to come back and perch in whenever he bl-blooming well feels like it? I'm sick and tired of pouring money into a place you and I never see—never want to see again! What we get from those people barely covers taxes and repairs!"

"Yes, I know all that, dear, but what shall I tell them? They'd better get the sweep in from the village, I suppose—"

"Yes, by all means."

"And perhaps the tree really ought to come down, if—"

"Certainly not. It's one of the oaks." George severely inspected the tray which Hinton was placing on the table beside him. "Thank you," he added in the same menacing tone, as she went. "I ask you—the butcher's boy!" said George.

" '—constitutes a serious danger,' " his mother was reading from the letter in her hand, " 'as it overhangs the road and the hedge and completely obscures the view from the left as you leave the drive.' After all, if a real accident should happen, we should feel to blame—"

"I certainly should not feel to blame, unless I was driving the car when it happened," said George, measuring out gin lavishly. "Alice is late, as usual."

Hilary was taking it all in from near the door, his always errant fancy thoroughly tickled now by this private view of his amusing family. Since he was no longer one of them, they had become like people in a play, which he observed from an impersonal seat in the front row. His mother he thought really delightful, a bit on the Marie Tempest side. As for George, it was not just his liver that wanted watching, it was his waistline. George was definitely "putting on," as they say in the country, and needed a trainer. A rough light gray suit did nothing for him, either, and as usual his necktie was a thing to scare the birds with. Hilary, whose dark hair and eyes and lean, boyish build were all from the other side of the family, would have advised his brother not to dress like a prosperous ruddy comedian, and who was his tailor anyhow?

"Man can spend half his life waiting for Alice to turn up," muttered George, pouring out a spoonful of the White Lady into a glass and tasting it with horrible grimaces because it was not yet iced.

"*What's that got to do with you, old boy?*" Hilary wanted to know, and as nothing further was likely to be got from George on the subject he turned to his mother and approached her at the writing-desk, deliberately striving to break through to her consciousness. "*Mother. Mother, listen to me. What's going on here? Is George double-crossing me?*"

"I'd hate to know," remarked George over the cocktails, "what her hairdressing bill comes to for the year."

"*You'll find out if you're not careful,*" Hilary told him.

"I suppose it's worth it," reflected George gloomily, and sampled the White Lady again.

Their mother had laid down the letter and sat watching George with her chin in her hand.

"George," she said suddenly, as though making up her mind, "you needn't think I haven't noticed, because I have."

"Noticed what, old lady?" said George, bluffing.

"You're in love with Alice. I'm your mother and I can tell."

"*Ah, here we go,*" said Hilary with satisfaction. "*How about it, George?*"

"You're much too clever, aren't you, mum? Besides, she's always run after Hilary, ever since they were kids."

"I know," she agreed gravely. "I never could understand it."

"*Couldn't you, dear?*" said Hilary, with rueful laughter.

George was looking self-conscious and pleased.

"Bless you, mum, you *are* partial, aren't you!"

"Oh, George, you ought to know by now that you're my favorite son—"

"*There you are, George, that's plain enough!*" The private view had taken a slightly unexpected turn, but Hilary was still an interested spectator. It was not really news to him that George was the favorite, he had known it at the back of his mind ever since their school days. But all the same, it was odd to hear her say it, so shamelessly, and to see how unsurprised George was. George had always known it too, obviously. Well, there was one thing about old George, he never pretended. It was like George to accept his mother's tribute with a frank pleasure amounting to smugness, and even to consider it no more than his due. Doubtless George was capable also of numbering Alice among his just prerogatives. He had the fine, lusty, open-faced ego of the pampered British male.

"You may think I don't think of these things, but I do," his mother went on to assure George seriously. "And that's why I know Hilary isn't the marrying kind, and the sooner Alice finds that out the better!"

"Yes, but in the meantime—until she does find out—I can't very well interfere, you know," George reminded her virtuously.

"Oh, you men!" she cried in exasperation. "When will you understand that a woman wants to be *won!*"

"Uh—I see," said George, and was visibly turning things over in his mind.

"*Careful, mother, you're giving him ideas*," Hilary cautioned her.

"You needn't look so innocent, George, you weren't born yesterday!" said his mother, and both her sons regarded her with amazement and no little respect, from their separate viewpoints. "I don't believe Hilary cares tuppence about Alice anyway," she remarked defiantly.

"She thinks he does," said George. "It amounts to the same thing."

"No—it doesn't," she contradicted. "Besides, she wouldn't be happy with him. I mean—" she added quickly, and then hesitated. "—that is—I don't think she would," she finished lamely.

"*Why?*" demanded Hilary.

George was silent, fiddling with the cocktail tray in an embarrassed sort of way, for he had not been on these confidential terms with his mother for years. She went to drawing little meaningless things on a fresh sheet of note-paper, taking care not to look at him, for she flattered herself that she never tried to interfere in her children's private affairs. Hilary came nearer to her, moving soundlessly across the carpet. Indirectly, she had answered him once before. Indirectly she seemed to be aware of him, and out of this wholly subconscious contact he hoped to glean the clues he needed, and perhaps find out why he was here instead of tucked up in his cozy grave on the Frontier.

"*What makes you say I couldn't have made her happy?*" he pressed her, his eyes fixed on her face which was bent above her wandering pen. "*How do you know?*"

"*I* wasn't—very happy," said his mother just above a whisper, watching the busy point of her pen. "And Hilary's exactly like his father."

That jerked George out into the open.

"Oh, here, I say—! I always thought you and the guvnor hit it off together fairly well—" he exclaimed, shocked.

His mother bit her lip, and drew a row of little circles on the paper and then went along the line putting dots in the center of each one, tidily. George was staring at her, the ice-tongs in his hand.

"I shouldn't have said anything," she murmured at last, very low. "I was only trying to help you, George."

"But of course, mum—say anything you like! Only—" George put down the ice-tongs, poured out half a glass of the White Lady, and drank it up.

"It's me you're trying to help," Hilary told her a bit grimly. *"You remember me, don't you, mother—I'm the younger one."*

"—only it was a bit of a shock!" said George, setting down the glass.

"Yes, I suppose it was," she admitted, connecting the row of circles with little rows of dots. "Of course we never—never *quarreled*, you know. And he never—never *threw* things at me!" The corners of her mouth deepened in her still girlish smile. "But—" She became absorbed in the minute gyrations of her pen.

"But what?" insisted Hilary, standing quite close to the desk now. *"You've got to clear this up. Why wouldn't I have made a good husband? What's wrong with me—and with my father?"*

"I certainly don't remember any rows," said George, without humor.

"Oh, no. There weren't any rows." She shook her head sadly. "Maybe if I'd kicked up a fuss sometimes—" Her voice drifted away. She never once looked towards her astonished elder son in the middle of the room.

"What was wrong with him?" asked George. "Those trips he made—was it other women?"

"Oh, goodness, no!" She laughed at him, but secretively, and would not meet his eyes. "I never had to worry about *that!*" she told her pen-point happily. "I didn't mean Hilary won't be *faithful* to her!"

"Oh," said George, frankly puzzled.

"*Thank you,*" said Hilary punctiliously. "*Just what did you mean, if you don't mind?*"

She gave a guilty sort of glance over her shoulder, as though to make sure that only George was in the room, and her voice dropped still lower.

"I'm—saying whatever comes into my head this morning, George, because I love you, and I want you to be happy. And I'd like to see Alice have what I never had—security, and a *settled* feeling. You see, George, you're not strictly a Shenstone. You're my own son, I always think, from the McAndrews side. You'd make Alice a good husband and father to her children, which is more than I can say for Hilary, and that's the truth. It wouldn't be the wretched, one-sided sort of thing I had to put up with all my life—while your father was alive—" Her voice broke suddenly, and she rested her head on her left hand, shielding her face.

Hilary made an instinctive move towards her, but George was there first, putting clumsy arms round her shoulders. He couldn't remember when he had last seen her cry.

"Here, hold on," he said. "For heaven's sake, old lady—!"

She clung to him, weeping.

"I—I don't know quite what's come over me this morning. I know I shouldn't be saying these dreadful things out loud. But it's not fair, George, it's not fair to Alice that I love like my own daughter, not to warn her! I don't want her to live as I had to live, always in deadly fear that her man won't come back—and the rest of the time hoping, *praying* that he won't go away again! And always knowing that it's no use, that he's bound to be off again soon—so soon—"

"But, mum, good Lord, you had the War," George reminded her futilely.

"It wasn't just during the War, George. Even before that started, he was always doing something for the Home Office that nobody else dared to do. Once he went to Russia about spies. Once he was down in Limehouse for six days and nights without sending me one word. Once they sent him to Egypt, and I didn't hear for two months—like Hilary now, out there on the Border. It's no marriage, it's no life for a woman—to love people like Hilary! Don't let her, George," she entreated him hysterically. "Don't *let* Hilary have Alice!"

"*I see*," said Hilary.

"Mater, for heaven's sake—!" George was genuinely horrified. "You really must pull yourself together!"

"Hullo, am I late or anything?" said Alice from the doorway. She saw Mrs. Shenstone's tears then, and halted with a child's embarrassed impulse to back out of the room, followed by a quick anxiety. "Oh, sorry—Hinton said—. What is it? Have you had bad news?"

"No, of course not—no news at all." Mrs. Shenstone recovered quickly, and wiped her eyes. "Come in, dear—you're not a bit late. George is going to make some cocktails. Luncheon will be ready in a minute. I must just go and see about the flowers—"

She hurried away, blowing her nose briskly as she went.

VIII

HILARY'S impulse too was to escape from the room now. He had had a few revelations, certainly, and he was pretty sure that more would follow if he remained where he was. He reminded himself that of course he was outside all the laws now. What he did now didn't matter. Or did it?

Suppose Alice didn't know that she had only just missed making a mistake—the same sort of mistake his mother had made. Suppose even after she was free, she failed to take the proper advantage of her release. Could he still influence her somehow, if he tried? Apparently he could get through to people a little—make them answer him, badger them into saying things they wouldn't ordinarily say, leave them forever wondering why they had spoken as they did. Perhaps with practice he would get better at it. Perhaps he had a power which was really worth cultivating—the power of disturbing people's minds from within, so that they thought things out a little differently than if they were allowed to go on fooling themselves. He wondered how far it would work.

Was George the right one for Alice, after all? Just how did she feel about George? If he had come back from

India in the usual way he might never have known. He had the chance to know now—to know exactly where he stood—would have stood, that is. It was a desolate thought as he faced it, that he might learn more about Alice in the next five minutes than if they had lived out the rest of their lives together. . . .

She stood looking after his mother—slim and straight and fair and desirable, her pale gold hair gleaming in sculptured curls round her halo hat. Her make-up was always exquisite, and the familiar fragrance which always clung about her reached him where he stood. She was lovely—lovelier than he had ever realized before it was too late. If he had come home on leave this summer, and found her looking like this, surely he would have had the good sense to urge a date for their wedding? And what would she have said to that—now that George had come into it? He felt he had to know.

George had dumped the ice into the White Lady hastily and was now performing tunes with the shaker as though the accumulation of frost on its outside was the most important thing in the world to him. And perhaps it was.

"*Carry on, George. Now's your chance. Who's stopping you?*" suggested Hilary.

"What upset her?" Alice was asking. "I thought perhaps she was worrying about Hilary again."

"No," said George, and began to pour out into the little stemmed glasses with great care. "Are you?"

"Well, I'm afraid I haven't been writing much either,"

she acknowledged defensively, "so I don't really deserve to hear. One loses touch." She accepted her glass from him and raised it, with a little provocative smile. "Cheerio," she said, and drank.

"Bung-ho," said George, and took his at a gulp.

"*Happy landings,*" murmured Hilary, watching them.

"Alice—" George set down his glass with a clink. "—how much longer are you going to let things go on like this?"

"What?" She raised startled blue eyes to his darkening gaze.

"How much longer are you going to let me dangle?"

"George, you're not to talk like that. Especially when we don't even know where Hilary is."

"*Oh, does that matter?*" queried Hilary.

"Does that make a difference?" said George.

"I don't know," she admitted unhappily. "I suppose it does."

"Very well. When he turns up the next time—"

"No, George, I won't listen!"

"You've got to listen. I'm sick of hanging about on one foot waiting for Hilary to make up his mind to marry you!" cried George angrily. "After all—where do I come in?"

"George, Hilary's never asked me to promise anything —actually. But if I choose to consider myself pledged—"

"Pledged to what?" he jeered rudely. "To marry him if and when he asks you to set a date, and then sit down in a vile hill station in India while he disappears on some comic-opera secret-service job and—"

"There's nothing comic about India just now."

"Then why go there?"

"I never said I was going there. Don't let's quarrel, George, least of all about Hilary."

"I'm not quarreling," asserted George. "I'm only asking you what there is in it for you as things are?"

She turned away, setting down her empty glass.

"Nothing," she said quietly. "Nothing very much."

"Then why do you go on with it?" demanded George logically.

There was a silence while she drifted down the room, avoiding chairs and tables blindly, her hands pressed together.

"*Tell him,*" Hilary directed her urgently. "*I want to know.*" But still she did not speak, staring down into the street from beside the window, moving on again, aimlessly, out of George's reach. "*Why did you go on with it?*" Hilary repeated.

"All right, George, I'll tell you," she said at last, and would not look round. "I'm sorry for him."

"Sorry for Hilary!" cried George in honest astonishment.

"*Sorry—!*" said Hilary, for it was one thing he had not thought of.

"Since your father died he's been so—so sort of solitary," she tried to explain. "He counts on me. I'm left over from the old days. I listen to him. I always have.

He's one of the last romantics, George, and nobody listens to them these days."

"*Well, I asked for that one!*" Hilary admitted. "*And I got it! Tell me more.*"

"Are you in love with him?" demanded George, coming after her, so that she turned to face him, at bay against the grand piano. George was in for it now, and he felt a cad, and all those things, but in a way he was glad too that the thing had got out of hand. He couldn't stop now, he was going to the bottom of it, and the hell with everything. After all, it was Alice's life too, as well as his own. Alice was not as young as she had been, dash it all, even if she did come in from the hairdresser's fit to dazzle a man entirely, smelling like flowers, and looking as though she'd break if you squeezed her. Alice wouldn't break. Not with that figure. . . . "*Are* you?" he demanded again, as she didn't answer, and his neck had got rather red.

"*Are you, Alice?*" insisted Hilary softly.

"I was." She hesitated. "I—could have been. Oh, don't let's talk about it!"

"Yes, we *will* talk about it!" said George obstinately and seized her by the elbows, and then, having gone so far, seemed a little at a loss.

"*That's the stuff, George,*" Hilary encouraged him promptly. "*You have it out with her. I want to know where I am!*"

"I suppose I'm not a romantic," George began hesitantly, "but I want you to be in love with me, Alice. I want it damnably. It was always Hilary with you, I knew that, and like a fool I stood back. My kid brother—and so on! Learned it at school. Well, I've finished with that. I've outgrown it, shall we say. Anyway, the kid brother stuff was tommyrot—Hilary was old before he was born! Able to take care of himself. Self-sufficient!"

"You're wrong," she said quietly. "That's just his shell."

"Shell be damned!" His hold on her tightened cruelly. "It's my turn now. I want you. Alice—you're wasting your life. I want you!"

"*Don't bully the girl, George*," Hilary advised him.

"I've let Hilary count on me," she was arguing gently. "He's confided in me, always. I've written him letters. I'm not going to let him down now."

"And what about me?" he asked with sudden humility.

"You?" She tried to laugh it off. "You'll be all right! You've heaps of friends. But Hilary's all alone. He needs me."

"*So that's how it is*," said Hilary, and he had never thought of it quite that way before.

"But—you'd rather it was me?" George persisted hopefully.

"We won't go into that now."

"Yes, we will!" He bent to look into her averted face. "You'd rather it was me—wouldn't you!"

"All right—" she sighed. "Suppose I would rather it was you. What then?"

"This," said George thickly, and kissed her hard.

For a moment she was quiet in his arms. Then she pulled away.

"We can't do this. I won't go back on Hilary. Not like this. At least not till I can talk to him—try to explain—"

"*You don't have to,*" said Hilary.

"You've a right to get on with your own life, Alice," George reminded her. "And you belong to me."

"It's not as simple as that."

"Maybe not for Hilary. He always does everything the longest way round!"

"*Not this time,*" said Hilary. "*You win, George. I lose. Get on with it.*"

Alice drew back, looking up at George with troubled eyes. His kiss had left her pulses pounding, she liked the desperate clasp of his arms round her, she liked being wanted so much. Thirty was looming over Alice, and her mother had begun to hint that if she wanted the right sort of marriage, with children and a place of her own, she had better make up her mind soon. She did want all those things—badly. It was flattering to her hungry feminine ego to have a man like George turn so recklessly impatient after dangling so long. It was stirring to feel one's power as a woman like this, and to know that one's looks weren't going off, at least not yet, and that one had only to say the word, for a very decent sort of wedding. And one could be proud of George, he had enough money, he was very masculine in a showy sort of way—and he wanted her. That was the most exciting part. He wasn't being very subtle about it, perhaps, but he would take her tomorrow if he could get her. . . .

"You're not behaving very well about this, George," she began uncertainly, feeling her way towards surrender.

"I'm tired of behaving well," he said brutally. "There's not much in it."

"I ought to resent your going for me like this—" She turned from him with a sigh.

"Do you know why you don't? Because you're only human, like the rest of us. Because I'm *here*—and I'm staying here—and I want you so much. More than he ever has, Alice—or he would have done something about it long ago. Enough to wait—how long have I waited?—ever since you were a kid. I gave Hilary a fair chance, I swear I did. He could have married you a dozen times over by now, if he'd wanted to."

She winced at that.

"You needn't rub it in."

"I suppose I'm saying a lot of unpardonable things," he admitted handsomely. "Hilary's old-fashioned soul would be scandalized. He might even have the cheek to deny that he didn't care enough about you to stay in England and try to make you happy. Well, he can deny it till the cows come home, but the fact remains, he hasn't done it! Stop playing the faithful maiden all forlorn, Alice—and have me instead!" He kissed her again, roughly, compellingly, holding her crushed against him till resistance went out of her, and then kissing her again, more gentle with conquest.

"I must see Hilary first—" she murmured weakly, leaning against him, glad of the hard, heavy feel of his shoulders under her hands, giddy with his candid need of her.

"You'd rather it was me," he repeated. "You said so."

"Did I?" She rested passive in his eager hold, but the blood was singing in her ears. "You're easier. I know where I am, with you. You're more comfortable—not so nervy—not so hard to live up to. If I did something you didn't like, you'd make a row and get it over. If I betrayed you, you'd knock me down—wouldn't you?"

"I would," he nodded, pleased with her.

"Hilary would just break his heart over it," she said. "For years I've been afraid of putting a foot wrong with Hilary. I'm terrified of him half the time. I never know quite what he wants, I can only try to do what he seems to expect of me, and hope for the best. I'm simply terrified to marry Hilary—but I'll never let him down if I can help it."

"You're going to let him down, my girl, if that's what you call it, whether you want to or not," George asserted flatly.

"George—please—" But as she straightened against his encircling arms, she felt them tighten possessively. She was helpless, mastered, prisoner to his great strength which enclosed her. "George, you're hurting me—"

"You like it. I know women," said George, perhaps a

little tactlessly, "they need something to hit against. Hilary's been too soft with you. I'll show you where you belong—"

She set her two hands against his massive shoulders and strove with all her might, while he looked down at her, smiling, and gave way no more than granite. With a gasp of laughter she surrendered, and her mouth was willing against his. . . .

Well, well, thought Hilary, enlightened, as he turned away towards the door—so George knows women, does he. And it looks as though he does, at that. She never kissed me that way. . . .

But as he reached the threshold, his mother was coming along the passage hurriedly, a crumpled paper in her hand. Oh, Lord, he thought, here's the Home Office, at last.

"George!" Mrs. Shenstone called sharply as she came. "Alice—George—where are you—" She stood in the doorway, her eyes blind with tears, her lips atremble.

"What is it, mater?" George went to her quickly.

"Darling, what's happened?" Alice's arms went round her on the other side.

"It's Hilary—I've had a telegram—"

"What about him, mater?"

"No—oh, *no—!*" cried Alice, looking frightened.

"He's dead." She collapsed into sobbing, and they led her to a chair near the table. George poured out a cocktail and held the glass firmly while she sipped at it and was calmer. Alice slid to her knees beside Mrs. Shenstone's chair and stayed there, staring straight ahead of her with wide, dry eyes.

A moment more Hilary lingered in the doorway, looking back at them. There was nothing for him to do here, Alice would find her own way to happiness now with no further help from him. I'm well out of that, he told himself firmly, resolutely denying himself sympathy as a jilted man. There was never much in it, I suppose, and now that George has learned about women . . . !

"*You're free, Alice,*" he said gently, hoping to make it a little easier. "*Don't start having a conscience now, for heaven's sake. You're free to marry George, without having to throw me over. Just what you wanted—or isn't it? Good luck, George—no hard feelings.*"

He kept on his way towards the stairs, through the empty hall, out into the sunlit street. . . .

Alice leaned her arms across Mrs. Shenstone's lap and hid her face from them both. Alice was thinking in a dazed, foolish way that there was a smear of lipstick still on George's chin—and remembering how Hilary used to pass a white handkerchief across his smiling mouth when they had sat out a dance in the garden, or—and how once she had said to him indignantly, "*My* lipstick doesn't come off on people!" and he had shown her his handkerchief, faintly smudged with pink, and laughed. And now she saw clearly all at once that Hilary had forgotten more about women than George would ever know—George, who boasted of his omniscience and was clumsy with his kissing. If ever once she had let herself go with Hilary as she had done today with George, instead of raising up a maidenly reserve between them in order to bait him into pressing for more—instead of hurling her virginity in his face in an effort to jockey him into marrying her—Hilary's thin brown hands—Hilary's lips, firm and sweet, but knowing, in their infrequent kisses—Hilary—gone—forever. . . .

"It was a shock," his mother was saying apologetically. "I—I never meant to break down like that, I—" Her eyes were fixed on George's stupefied face. "What is it, George? Why do you look so—queer? George, what are you thinking?"

"Nothing," he said, looking very queer indeed. "Nothing, only—it was Hilary's room old Ponsonby had last night at the club."

IX

HILARY found himself again in the sunny street, drifting aimlessly. So Alice would marry George and be happy—happier than his mother had been. He realized, now that she had brought it home to him, that it was no life he would have offered a wife. But he had promised himself to settle down one day, perhaps at Nuns Farthing. He had never meant to die in his tracks like that, on the wrong side of the Frontier. If Alice had played her cards right, he might never have gone back to India. . . .

But Alice was afraid of him, and that was the lack of perfection he had always acknowledged privately in their long association. She was never really at ease with him. How awful if they had married and she had gone on feeling like that. Never sure, she said, exactly what he wanted. He had supposed that he wanted much the same sort of thing as other men—surely he had demonstrated that already, once or twice—but Alice had sensed a difference somewhere. And after taking another good look at George, he thought he saw. George must look simple enough, even to Alice. George had said with some satisfaction that he was not a romantic. But where would

George be now without the few romantics who were still trying to hold the world together so that the Georges could go on living unmolested in their smug houses?

Anyway, Alice would have what she wanted soon, with no help from him. Alice was not his job. There was something else . . . something waiting . . . somewhere. . . .

Paddington Station was just ahead of him. At sight of it, confusion vanished. Nuns Farthing. They had let it, with his room just as he had walked out of it that day two years ago. Of course they must have left the door locked. If they hadn't he would see that they heard about it. If anyone had been allowed to go mucking about with his things . . .

That was it! Strangers were in possession down there. He had to get back. As for those people who had let the house and were living there, he could easily turn them out. A few manifestations, a few things going bump in the night, and they would pack up and leave, and he would have the place to himself again.

I suppose an old hand at this game would know how to get there without the railway, he thought, entering the booking-hall. Perhaps in a hundred years' time I'll learn how to transport myself through space on my own. But until I get the hang of it—well, anyway, I don't need a ticket.

A train for Wells was leaving in ten minutes. Smiling, he slid past the man at the barrier and went down the platform where doors stood open all along the train. He chose a first-class non-smoking compartment as being likeliest to remain empty, and settled himself in the near corner seat with his back to the engine. This is doing the company out of twenty-four and ninepence, he thought with satisfaction.

"'Ere you are, ma'am—No Smoking—'nk you, ma'am!"

A porter swung a neat dressing-case to the rack over Hilary's head, assisted a nice old lady up the step, and pocketed his tip.

She was frail and beautifully dressed and smelt of violets; the sort of old lady who always has the corner seat with her back to the engine. Hilary slid hastily along the upholstery or she would have sat down on him. He wondered what it would have been like, for both of them, if she had, and wondered too if he would ever have the courage to make such experiments, and decided that the sooner he got into a quiet life at Nuns Farthing the better.

For something over two hours he and the old lady traveled in silence, across the June countryside. No one disturbed them.

But as they neared the little station of Upper Bramble, near Wells, he perceived uneasily that she was not going to get out first. Reluctantly, therefore, when the train slowed to a stop he pulled himself together, seized the latch, and jumped out as the door swung open under his hand. A bored, unseeing country porter slammed it shut again, unaware of her astonishment.

Yellow sunset light still touched the tops of the trees at the end of the long midsummer day, but the hedged lane grew dusky as he walked the two miles between the station and Nuns Farthing. A couple of motor cars and a boy on a Walls bicycle passed him without incident.

Only a short way from the gates he met a farmer with a dog at his heels, trudging towards the pub at Upper Bramble. As they came level the dog shied into the ditch and stood there, stiff-legged, growling in its throat, while the hair on its back rose.

"Come on, then, you silly fool," said the farmer over his shoulder.

"*Good evening*," said Hilary politely at a venture, and the dog let out an hysterical yelp.

"What's the matter wi' ye, Nab—seein' things?" grinned its master, and the dog hurried after him, still growling, into the dusk.

Hilary had to admit to himself that he was shaken by the encounter. It was a new and humiliating sensation to him to be barked at by a dog as though he was a tramp —only worse. Normally he had got on with dogs. Heretofore they had always smiled at him and thrust damp friendly muzzles into his hand if encouraged. It was no fun to be outlawed by dogs, it was as though a door had opened somewhere between the worlds and a cold draught was blowing through. That dog had seen him, there was no doubt about it. And the farmer had not. Either way, it was wrong. Horses, too, he surmised, would have none of him now. He began to feel as though there wasn't going to be much left. . . .

It was nearly dark when he reached the house, and lights showed in some of the windows. His footsteps quickened at sight of it, and a feeling of restoration and achievement swept through him. He had come home. Nuns Farthing, at least, was still the same, and there was comfort in it, there would be privacy and solace within his own four walls. Books. He could still read books. And no one would care what he did in his own room at the top of the house, there would be no one to see. . . .

Once more he was confronted with the problem of a closed door, for the evening was cool.

There must be a way to pass through a door without opening it, he told himself, but I'm hanged if I see my way to try it now.

He walked round the house to the back, noticing with approval that the garden was well-kept and flourishing. A mounting excitement had begun to possess him, as though some tremendous experience was drawing nearer with every step he took; an exhilaration out of all proportion to the obvious satisfaction it would be to see his own things again and make sure that all was well with them.

It's coming, he thought, trying not to hurry foolishly, for surely there was no need for him to hurry ever again? Whatever it is, it's going to happen now. I was wasting time in Town—not that time matters after all. But this is it. This is what I've been headed for. I might have known it was here, all along. It's coming now—whatever it is. . . .

Through the kitchen window he could see Mrs. Pilton, sitting as she used to do, with her knitting. The maids must be out courting in the summer twilight, or had got a lift in to the cinema. For a moment he paused to contemplate the dark, brooding face bent above her knitting, while a grateful feeling of companionship crept through his loneliness and his driving anxiety. This strange, uncommunicative woman, a native of the grim countryside, was part of his childhood. She had changed very little since his earliest memory of her.

As far back as he could go, she had been a widow, with a somber immobility of expression occasionally lighted up by a smile which wrought a dazzling change in her, showed white, even teeth and golden flecks in her dark eyes. He was unaware, even now, that that fleeting glimpse of lost beauty which lived in her smile was his own personal property, and had never once been seen by George; though he was not so stupid as not to suspect as time went on that here, at least, he was the favorite.

In all the years he had known her, he had learned almost nothing of her life beyond where it touched his own. What her days had held before she came to Nuns Farthing, whom she had loved, what death might have taken from her to leave her solitary, what she had dreamed of, what she might still hope for—it was all unknown to him. But for his part, he had told her almost nothing of his own accomplishments and adventures away from Nuns Farthing. Travelers' tales were not part of their inarticulate reunions, even as she had never once said to him—"When I was a girl—" They had existed always in a fourth dimensional present, which took no account of time or the outside world, and which had endured from the old days when, just home from school, he had perched on a stool in the kitchen waiting for the lemon curd to cool, down to his last return but one, when she had tended him faithfully—but for the most part silently—through a bad backfire of fever. Undemonstrative, inarticulate, indestructible, their strange friendship stretched back the whole length of his memory, and never once had she let him down.

Even if she had known he stood there watching her now, even if she knew he had come back, like this, seeking sanctuary in the house, she was not the sort to scream, or shrink from his invisible presence. The sight of her was boundlessly comforting in his bewilderment. If she would stay on when the others were gone, as they were sure to go, after he took up his residence here . . .

Hardly knowing what he expected, he went to the kitchen door and tried the handle. It was locked for the night. He knocked on the panels softly—and heard her moving to let him in, watched the door open before him into the lighted room. She stood there, tall and calm and unfrightened, while he crossed the threshold into the kitchen.

"So you've come back at last," she said quietly.

He stared at her.

"I can't see you, Master Hilary, but I know you're there. I've felt you homing ever since nightfall." She closed the door and locked it again, without once looking in his direction, and returned to her chair and took up her knitting. "You'll find things just as you left them upstairs," she added, her eyes on her busy needles.

"Thank you, Mrs. Pilton." He lingered a moment hopefully. *"Can't you hear me?"* he ventured at last.

She made no answer.

A moment more he stood looking at her bent head, the small click of her needles audible in the stillness. Well, she had spoken to him, that was something. She, out of all the world, was aware of him and yet did not resent his presence. That was her Mendip breeding, the Hills were full of ghosts, they said. . . . Ghosts. He was able to smile at the word, often so lightly used by people who thought they were joking.

She had not failed him, even now. He could ask for nothing more. And still the divine unrest was dragging at him, urging him on, on, and the thing he was here for was very close now, he knew, almost under his hand. He opened the door into the pantry and passed through it into the darkened dining-room on his way to the stairs. Glancing back, he saw her rise to close the pantry door softly behind him.

As he reached the dimly lighted hall where the stairs were, a middle-aged woman with fluffy gray hair and innocent blue eyes was coming down the steps. A small fat dog ran on ahead of her and planted itself in the middle of the carpet facing him, in a tornado of hysterical barking.

"Bella, for goodness' sake, what *is* it?" cried Aunt Effie.

"*Shut up, you little beast*," said Hilary, for this was not a nice dog, not even an intelligent dog, and yet it was possessed of a dog's fundamental instincts and so undertook to bark at him in his own house because his presence there outraged its common-sense. "*Let it go, can't you? Shut up, I say!*" And he snapped his fingers at Bella, who retreated before him, her scruff on end, making rude noises in her throat.

"What *did* you think you saw?" chided Aunt Effie, gathering Bella into her arms. "There's nothing there, you foolish girl! See, Auntie's not afraid!"

From the shelter of Auntie's protective clasp, Bella gave several more sharp, high-pitched barks, and the study door opposite the stairs opened abruptly.

"Effie, what on earth ails that damned dog?" demanded Father from his threshold.

"I can't think!" said Aunt Effie apologetically, making ineffectual attempts to soothe Bella. "I was just coming down from Sabrina's room, and Bella got some sort of fright. Our little invalid has gone off to sleep nicely, Alan, I'm sure she'll be all right tomorrow."

"That's good. But a man can't hear himself think." The study door closed again.

What dreadful people, thought Hilary, mounting the

stairs. I can't have this. They must go. I'll see to that.

He realized that the dog Bella would make it ridiculously easy. A few judicious appearances at night—a few unaccountable occurrences—a slight poltergeist atmosphere—they would go fast enough, and the house would be closed again, and he would be left in peace among his own belongings, to work out whatever time—endless time—would bring to him.

Having come to the top of the first flight, he found himself pausing before the closed door of the blue room—the best guest room—the room Alice always had when she came to visit. Obedient to some irresistible necessity, careless of consequences, he turned the knob noiselessly and went in.

A night-light burned on the table by the bed, where a girl-child lay asleep, her lashes dark against pale cheeks, her fine golden brows a little drawn, her wide sweet mouth tightly closed, as though even in slumber she was beset by some unchildlike worry. He saw by the length of her, from the square, determined chin to the small mound made by her feet, that she must be well into her teens, for all the delicacy of the bare arm flung above her head, and the natural silk of her fair hair.

Fascinated, soothed, and possessed by a deep contentment he had never known before, he hung over the bed watching her breath come and go as she slept. Infinitely helpless she looked to him—defenseless, troubled, and pitiably young—Sabrina, the invalid, who had gone off to sleep so nicely.

And that futile woman with the dog, and the irate old man in the study doorway—were they all she had to look after her, and why hadn't they got at whatever it was that oppressed her and wiped it out? Why wasn't somebody sitting with her, if she was ill? Suppose she woke alone and was frightened. Suppose she called out. No one could hear. . . .

In her sleep she stirred and smiled, and groped with one thin hand for his, where it rested on the pillow as he bent above her. Incredulously he felt the warmth of her clinging fingers. But how could that be, when he could feel neither hunger nor fatigue. . . . Journey's end. . . .

He knelt beside the bed, her warm fingers cradled in his.

X

SABRINA woke to a darkened room, but the edges of the curtains were gilded with sunlight. Her bedside clock said ten minutes to nine. She slid out onto the floor without slippers or dressing-gown and went to pull back the curtains. The garden looked delicious in the morning light, its dominant color the singing blue of the first delphiniums in the border.

For a few minutes, kneeling on the window seat with her elbows on the sill, she wondered why it felt like such a special day, even more special than birthdays or Christmas. Something heavenly seemed about to happen.

Then she remembered the dream.

But the more she tried to capture the dream again, the more elusive it became. Something about his coming back—yes, that was it. She had dreamed he was here in the house. Perhaps there would be a letter in the morning post, for Father, of course, to say he was coming down to fetch something he had left behind. Or perhaps a car would just drive up and a strange man would get out, and that would be—oh, what *was* his name! Or perhaps—

The old magic reasserted itself in the same absorbing

game. He would come back. She would see him—speak to him, at last. Perplexing things would get straightened out in the light of his wisdom and experience. . . .

Cold water on her face, and the commonplace details of dressing dimmed the dream still more. But the feeling of expectancy persisted. Something had brought him suddenly nearer. Something was different. Something special. . . .

Father and Aunt Effie had nearly finished breakfast when she entered the dining-room.

"Darling!" cried Aunt Effie in astonishment, dropping the *Express*. "You shouldn't have got out of bed without letting me know! But how *well* you look this morning! Alan, I *said* she'd be better this morning, the way she went off to sleep last night! Look, Alan, you'd never know she'd been ill!"

"I knew it wasn't a chill on the liver," said Father, glancing at her round the *Times*. "She's much too young for such things. Upset stomach, that's what it was. Too much sweet stuff, no doubt. Fool of a doctor."

"I had a lovely sleep," said Sabrina, with a secret smile for the dream. "Nobody could stay in bed on a morning like this!" She kissed them both lightly, and went to inspect the sideboard hot-plates. "What can I have to eat?"

"I'll ask them to boil you a little egg," said Aunt Effie, and rang the bell.

"Oh, Auntie, can't I have some bacon or something with it? I'm hungry!"

"Do you hear that, Alan, she's hungry!"

"Kidneys," said Father, folding the *Times* and preparing to disappear into the study. "Kidneys, my girl, that's what you need. Make them feed you up. Too much of this eating off trays in bed!"

"There aren't any more kidneys," Sabrina discovered sadly at the sideboard. "There's some bacon left, though. I'll have some bacon."

"I think a nice soft-boiled egg for our invalid, Jennie," Aunt Effie was saying to the maid who stood smiling at Sabrina from behind Father's chair.

"And some hot toast, Jennie," pleaded Sabrina, carrying a plate with bacon on it to her place at the table. "I'm not an invalid any more."

"Yes, miss, I can see that!" beamed Jennie. "Shall I make fresh tea?"

Aunt Effie felt the pot anxiously. She was full of futile small economies.

"No, no, this is still *very* hot," she asserted. "This will be quite all right, I'll water it out a bit and it won't be too strong."

Jennie departed to the kitchen with the good news, and Sabrina accepted gratefully a cup of the watered tea. As she began on the bacon, which was still appetizing, she watched Father gather up a handful of letters beside his plate.

"Was there anything exciting in the post this morning, Father?" she inquired cunningly.

"Exciting?" He paused beside his chair and appeared to give the word careful consideration, but she knew it was only absentmindedness. "Well, yes, Professor Frinton has made a very interesting discovery in the gruffy-ground at Dolebury. Very. It is, of course, fantastic to say that the ancients built on the hilltops because they liked the view," he reminded them contentiously. "Dolebury was built for its lead-mines. Now that he has himself found flint on the spot, Frinton may begin to see reason, for he knows very well that there is no flint on Mendip. It was brought here for a purpose, by the long barrow men, a child could see that! Well, I shall drive over there this morning and hear what he has to say for himself."

"It's a lovely day for a drive." Sabrina sighed with open envy of anyone who was setting out into the blue and gold world.

Father sent a suspicious glance at what he could see of the day, through the open casements.

"Mmmmmm," he said conservatively. "Looks like thunder later. I shall take a mackintosh."

He escaped with his letters and the *Times*.

Sabrina sighed again, as the boiled egg arrived before her, accompanied by fresh hot toast in a china rack.

"You know, Auntie, it's a little frightening," she said, and brought the spoon down with a smart smack on the shell.

"What, dear—frightening?" Aunt Effie tore herself out of the astrology column in the *Express*. She was Virgo, and for Virgo people it was a good day for business ventures, and yellow was the lucky color.

"Father, I mean. He might as well be dead."

"Sabrina!"

"Well, I mean—a glorious morning like this, and he doesn't even notice till someone points it out, and then he remembers to take his mackintosh. Was Father ever young?"

"Well, dear, ever since your poor mother died—"

"Yes, I know, that must have been dreadful for him. But even if the person you love best in the world does die—and you are left behind—it's only a matter of time, isn't it, till you catch them up again."

"Well, darling, I think that sounds rather heartless," began Aunt Effie, with a vague doubt somewhere that it could be quite as simple as that. "And besides, you're much too young to—"

"I didn't mean it to sound heartless at all. I only meant that Father needn't—"

"Anyway, it's not a very cheerful subject for such a bright morning, is it!" Aunt Effie chided her playfully. "I think it would be nice if you took a little stroll in the warm sun—be sure to wear a hat, and wrap yourself up well, won't you—while I do the ordering. The snapdragons are coming out at last, the lazy things."

Well, there it was again. Father making off into his study as soon as he had finished feeding, Aunt Effie refusing to listen. Not, perhaps, that one had anything important to say, but one longed occasionally to stretch one's mind, to exercise one's imagination out loud, discussing things one didn't know much about. Else how was one to work things out for oneself, and find out how other people arrived at their own conclusions, and what these conclusions were?

In thwarted silence, Sabrina finished her boiled egg and bacon, two pieces of toast, well-buttered, decided against a second cup of lukewarm tea, and drifted out to the snap-dragons. Pale yellow, peach and pink and dark crimson, they stood in sturdy ranks along the border. She bent and pinched one to make it gape, detached a full-blown bloom from a pillar rose to pull through her belt buckle, and glanced up at the windows of the L-shaped room as she always did from that part of the garden. They were closed, of course.

All the bewildered mistrust of the room which had come upon her in the chill gray twilight of her last visit had vanished over night, and she was able now to lay it to the weather, or to her illness, whatever it was, coming on. The rain and her own feverish imagination had tricked her. She felt again, and welcomed, the old familiar fascination. She must go up there, at once. The room was lonely, and must be aired out on a day like this.

She ran into the house and up the stairs. In the upper passage she met the housekeeper with a pile of fresh linen over her arm, and said a gay good-morning in return for a grave smile. At the foot of the second flight she paused and looked back in time to see the woman enter her room, the blue room. Sabrina turned round on a sudden impulse, and followed.

"Mrs. Pilton, do you ever hear from the family that owns this house?"

The housekeeper was preparing to change the bed linen. She went on working, unhurried, calm, deft, stripping back the covers, folding the sheets neatly as she removed them.

"Not often," she said in her quiet voice. "The last time was when Mrs. Shenstone wrote to say your father had taken the house."

"Was that when she told you to lock the room upstairs and not let us use it?"

"Yes. That was in the letter too."

"She—she didn't say anything about when he might be coming back?"

"No. I don't think she knew."

"I had a queer dream last night. I dreamed that he did come back." It was out. She waited defensively, ready to shrivel if the woman laughed or tried to explain away so irrelevant a revelation, already wishing the words unspoken.

The housekeeper unfolded a clean sheet and shook it out, snowy and billowing. It settled slowly on the mattress, while a fresh whiff of lavender and linen hung in the air.

"Were you glad to see him?" she inquired gently, bending to tuck in the edges.

"Yes, I was." Excessive gratitude overflowed in Sabrina's heart. No ridicule here, and no opaque preoccupation, putting her off. "Only I didn't *see* him exactly.

I don't know what he looks like. I only felt he was here —in the dream, I mean. And I was glad because—well, I've got to know him rather well, through his room, you know. You don't really think he'd mind my going there, do you?"

There was a long silence, until she almost thought the woman had not heard, or would not answer. Then—

"Did he seem to mind, in your dream?"

"No. That is—I can't remember much about the dream, except a heavenly feeling that now everything had come right. Do you think that's a good omen?"

The housekeeper peeled a pillow expertly and inserted it into a fresh cover.

"It's done you a world of good, anyone can see that," she said.

"It was nice to feel he was near," said Sabrina seriously. "Perhaps it means that he really is coming back, and we shall hear something from him soon." The words hung there hopefully, but there was no answer. "I seem to know him so well now—he's turning into a sort of guardian angel. Does that sound silly to you?"

The woman straightened, the edge of the primrose blanket in her hands, the sweet smell of sun-dried linen between them, and their eyes met across Sabrina's bed.

"I should go on thinking of him like that, if I were you," she said, and added after a moment—"No matter what happens."

"Thank you. I thought you'd understand." With a

dazzling smile Sabrina left her, and went on up the stairs.

She was more than a little surprised at the impulse which had led her to confide in Mrs. Pilton like that, but the woman's quiet dignity was attractive and comforting. And she hadn't tried to laugh it off about the dream, or changed the subject as not suitable, or questioned one's right to dream about a man one had never seen. One had to talk to somebody once in a while, reflected Sabrina, thoughtfully mounting the stairs. If things went on like this, one would find oneself talking out loud to— There, she had missed another chance to ask Mrs. Pilton what his name was.

In the long, sunny room at the top of the house he heard her feet on the stairs. Then the door opened and she came in, wearing a blue dress, with a rose in her belt—taller than he had expected, and too thin. He stood up politely, beside the window seat from where he had been watching her in the garden.

He was not altogether unprepared to see her here, for he had found his door unlocked the night before. A hasty investigation had shown him that nothing had been moved. His desk was the same, his clothes were still there. At least no one was living in the room. Neither was there a two years' accumulation of dust. Someone came in and out, then, but left his things alone.

Sabrina paused just inside the door, and stood for a moment, the knob still in her hand, glancing about her with questioning eyes.

"Please come in," said Hilary from the window. *"You won't mind me, will you?"*

Sunlight streamed through the casements toward her, making diamond-shaped nuggets of warm gold on the floor. The blended reds and blues and greens and browns of books, carpets, and old polished wood were lovelier than ever before to her eager gaze. How silly she had been ever to feel frightened here. Everything in the room seemed to shine and glow with welcome. She ought to apologize to it for such foolishness.

"Hullo again," whispered Sabrina, shamefaced.

"Hullo," said Hilary, surprised.

Obviously quite unaware of him, full of housewifely purpose, she went to set the casement windows wide to the morning air, kneeling on the window seat to the left of him as she did so.

"There," she said with satisfaction, under her breath. "That's better." And she sat back on her heels against the cushions, her elbows on the sill, looking down into the garden and pondering something deep within her mind.

Hilary sat down cautiously on the other end of the window seat and watched her, wondering what was in her thoughts. He was infinitely grateful to her for this unconscious companionship, and dared to hope that his presence was not going to upset her or frighten her away. So far she had not noticed him at all, nor seemed to sense any difference in the room as she had grown accustomed to it. And then his hope darted ahead of that purely negative comfort. Even if she knew he was there—would she mind?

At last she spoke again, very low, to herself.

"I don't see why I shouldn't talk to him sometimes—up here," she said.

"Who, me?" said Hilary, delighted. *"Why not?"*

She went on brooding, her elbows on the sill, her eyes resting on the flower-studded garden below. Mornings like this, he seemed so near—especially today. After all, she reflected, people talked out loud to dolls and nobody thought that was queer. And after all, you prayed out loud and yet you didn't see God—or expect Him to answer so you could hear. . . . One sometimes wrote letters to people one didn't actually know, too. She had thought more than once of writing him a letter, about the room and—and about how she had come to feel about it. But even for a letter one needed to know his name, else George might get it, and one would hate that.

She turned her head slowly, and her eyes went dubiously round the room, blinking a little in the sunlight. If only there was a picture of him, it would seem more reasonable to pretend he was actually there and could hear if she spoke to him. Or if only one knew his name. . . . You couldn't live in a room all your life and not leave your name somewhere in it—or could you?

She cast a helpless, ingratiating look round the four walls again, as if seeking him. Where could one look? Would he mind very much if—?

"If I could find his name," she said wistfully, just

above a whisper, "I think I could talk to him—sometimes."

"My name is Hilary," he told her, with a sudden, aching desire that she should know it.

The feeling grew on him minute by minute as he watched her that some sixth sense of hers would surely hear him, that already her sensitive, childlike perception had picked up some impression of his nearness and that she was glad of it. Minute by minute he was surer that his presence in the room she had made sanctuary was not going to come as a shock to her, and the knowledge bred in him a high exhilaration like a wind from the sea. If Sabrina did not mind his being there, if his homecoming did not drive her away, then he was not after all exiled and alone.

She had risen and gone to the desk, and now she stood looking down at the blotter.

"There's that letter to Thompson," she murmured, "only he didn't sign it."

"The phone rang," he explained.

"I wonder who Thompson is."

"You wouldn't care for him," he told her from the window seat. *"He's a member of His Majesty's Opposition. He will probably see to it that questions are asked in the House about the very thing Dalton and I were trying to cover up."*

Delicately, with the tips of her fingers on the handle, she drew out the middle drawer of the desk. Paper clips—elastic bands—an artists' small transparent ruler and triangle, drawing materials of all kinds, a huddle of foreign coins in an uncovered box, a pen-knife, a bottle-opener, a cork-screw—she closed the drawer, disappointed, and opened the right-hand one. Piles of note-paper and envelopes—Edward VIII stamps.

"I know!" she said suddenly. "Handkerchiefs!"

As she approached the tall chest of drawers in the corner, she met Alice's level, sulky stare in the silver frame. To his intense amusement, without hesitation she lifted the frame and turned Alice's face to the wall. Then she opened the top left-hand drawer, glanced once at its contents and closed it hastily, and tried the next one.

Handkerchiefs, yes—a tidy pile, all marked with the letter H. No more.

"Not Henry," she said aloud. "I couldn't bear that! Nor Harold, either. What other H's are there?"

"*Hilary*," he insisted, moving towards her across the room. "*Do try to hear me, Sabrina. Hilary.*"

"Hector," she guessed wildly, and grinned. "How awful! Well, where else, I wonder?"

"*My blessed idiot, the inside breast pocket of a man's coat has his name on a label. Don't you know anything about us at all? Look in my coats in the wardrobe.*"

Such an unsatisfactory sort of person he was, anyway, she grumbled to herself as she turned away from the chest of drawers. No name—no face—no address— She had come again to the picture of little boys grouped on a lawn with a football, and she paused in front of it, staring at it hopelessly.

"Second from the right in the first row," he said over her shoulder, and pointed with his finger on the glass. *"That's me."*

She turned away with a sigh, laying a caressing hand on the panels of the wardrobe as she passed it.

"There you are," he said quickly. *"My coats."*

"He might have had a bookplate," she muttered, drifting discontentedly across the carpet. "But all he ever does is write 'Shenstone' inside the cover."

"It's in my Kipling," he said, following her. *"Surely you've had my Kipling off the shelf? My name's in every volume of the older ones. Look in my Kipling, Sabrina."*

She stood behind the chesterfield, scowling at the handsome rows of books in their open shelves which lined the walls. Didn't he ever win prizes at school? She never had, but other girls had been presented with Bibles or Jane Austen or Maria Edgeworth, with their own names actually printed on in real type, or else inscribed in a clergyman's flowing hand. Surely if he was a bright little boy, and showed up well when visitors came . . . Surely he was the right sort of little boy at school, and never made a fool of himself there, as she had done. . . .

"To your right, Sabrina—the other side of the mantelpiece—" He spoke urgently from the middle of the room behind her, motionless there, striving desperately now to reach her with some sense of his words. *"Those red and gold books on the second shelf to the right of the mantelpiece—they were all given to me by a dear maiden aunt*

with a vice for scribbling on fly-leaves, dates and all. Find my Kipling, Sabrina—"

She wavered, hung on one foot, moved vaguely towards the mantelpiece, and halted again, looking up at it disapprovingly.

"You might have won a golf trophy," she said, and this time it was a direct reproach, "or a tennis championship—or a steeplechase. Then they would have engraved your name on a lovely silver cup, and it would be here on the mantelpiece for me to read. I can't think what you've done with your time."

"*Wasted*," he said, watching her from the middle of the room, awed and paralyzed by that first unconscious "you." "*All wasted, till today! Keep to your right, Sabrina—that's it—you're getting warm now—the Kipling, Sabrina, you can't miss it—no, the shelf above that one—above it—up one, I tell you, you must hear me—red and gold—higher, my darling, higher—*"

Her feet had carried her forward uncertainly. Her hand came up, hovered, and fell on *Puck of Pook's Hill*.

"*Got it!*" cried Hilary with infinite satisfaction, from the middle of the room.

She lifted the book off the shelf and opened it, turning the leaves lovingly.

"Did you read this when you were little, I wonder?" she murmured. "I did, more than once. It would be fun to read it again—together."

"*My name's in the front of it, Sabrina, in Aunt*

Dorothy's handwriting. I know it's damn' silly what she wrote, but you've got my name in your hands—"

The well-worn pages flipped back slowly under her thumb—

> " 'And see you, after rain, the trace
>   Of mound and ditch and wall?
> O that was a Legion's camping-place,
>   When Caesar sailed from Gaul,' "

she read aloud, in a glow of rediscovery. "But of course! That's what living in London does to you! I never realized before—it's all round this house—Maesbury Camp, where Father goes—Dolebury, too—mound and ditch and wall—*traces*—"

"*Go on,*" he said compellingly, from where he stood, hungry for the sound of the dear, remembered words. "*You're in the midst of it here, didn't you know? Please go on, Sabrina—*"

> " 'And see you marks that show and fade,
>   Like shadows on the Downs?
> O they are the lines the Flint Men made
>   To guard their wondrous towns.
>
> " 'Trackway and Camp and City lost,
>   Salt marsh where now is corn;
> Old Wars, old Peace, old Arts that cease—
>   And so was England born!' "

Her voice faltered on the last line, and she stood looking down blindly at the page where his own eyes had misted many a time.

> " '*She is not any common Earth,*
> *Water or wood or air,*' "

he prompted, but Sabrina carried the book to the chesterfield and sat down there, one foot beneath her.

"I shall have to read it all again," she was saying, her face alight and eager. "I shall have to get out on the hills—I want to see for myself—shadows on the Downs—"

The cover, loosened from much use, fell open, away from the writing on the fly-leaf. Her eyes widened as she read.

" 'To darling Hilary on his 12th birthday, with fondest love from his Auntie Dot. September 6, 1916.' " She gave a little gasp of triumph and excitement, and read the words again unbelievingly. "Why, that's it! I've found you!" And she repeated thoughtfully—"Hilary."

"*That's it,*" he said, watching her. "*Do you like it?*"

"Hilary," she said again softly. "It's perfect. It couldn't have been anything else. And it was Puck who told me. How queer."

"*You heard me!*" he marveled. "*You must have heard me—in a way. I can get through to you. Perhaps with practice I can make you know all the things I want to tell you—because you found your way to me here. It's rather—sobering—to me.*"

She had pulled a pillow into place behind her back and begun to read, becoming instantly absorbed. Hilary went back to the window seat and sat down there, glad that he knew the book so well that he could almost follow her progress through it from across the room. The first story was about Weland the Smith, and there was that nice bit about sacrifices. . . .

He had a good deal to think about, as they sat together through the lazy June morning. He would have come back to England, he was thinking, in the ordinary course of events, some time later in the summer—about the middle of August. He would have come down to Nuns Farthing at once to see about his room. He and Sabrina would have met then—those clear gray eyes, that wide, engaging smile, the warm little fingers—her implicit confidence in the man who belonged to this room. . . . He would have had to exercise patience—she was so young—but she was his, and he liked to think he would not have been clumsy, or hurried her. . . .

Obviously, whenever, however, he came, he was to find her here waiting for him. But it oughtn't to be like this. Something had gone wrong, out there on the Frontier. It was never meant to be like this. . . .

XI

A FEW days later Sabrina sat dozing in a deck-chair on the lawn, while Aunt Effie moved along the herbaceous border snipping faded blooms into a basket. It was nearly five. They were waiting for tea to come out to the table laid under a big tree.

The white lace cloth stirred in a languid breeze, the silver tray and flowered Worcester china glinted with shifting flecks of sunlight which fell through the whispering leaves above. A bowl of strawberries and an uncut cake had already arrived but were as yet undiscovered by any contentious wasp. Striped deck-chairs and bright chintz cushions, Sabrina's blue and white frock, echoed the riotous color in the sunlit border where Aunt Effie in apple-green linen administered to a clump of snapdragons.

Nuns Farthing drowsed in a peacefulness not of this bustling world, under a midsummer magic which seemed to hold time itself in thrall, so that the shadows forgot to creep across the grass and the sun delayed its evening plunge towards the treetops beyond the house.

Torpid with contentment and the pleasant contemplation of tea in the immediate offing, Sabrina lay back and watched through half-closed eyes a small, laggard cloud in a sky of almost tropical blueness, and wondered dimly how they had ever existed so long in a flat in London, with nothing to look at but walls, and nothing to do but eat and sleep and read books, or drift aimlessly in parks whose flowers all belonged to the King or the County and must not be picked, or even tended, by unauthorized persons. For years she had been buying flowers from barrows and shops, and often they were not fresh and died almost before she got them home. For years Aunt Effie had had no real occupation all day long, and now she was getting brown and positively plump from hours on her knees in the sun, digging and snipping and weeding. You read less in the country too, Sabrina was thinking in a rambling sort of way, half asleep in the deck-chair. You were less likely to be bored if you didn't, because there was always something to look at. You read less and dreamed more, and that must be good for you, in the long run, because you had time to invent thoughts of your own and get them sorted out into conviction, and philosophy, and possibly religion, without their getting buried under the miscellaneous printed opinions of other people.

Her mind went back, a long, long way, it seemed, to that night at dinner in London when Father first spoke of the house he had taken in the Mendip Hills—sprang it on them, without warning, and before anybody could say *Knife* he had dumped them down in it, bag and baggage, with the flat locked up in dust-sheets behind them, and nothing in the shape of a town nearer than Wells. Suppose they hadn't liked it at all, that wouldn't have mattered to Father, so long as he had his barrows and encampments, and his chosen cronies who drove with professorial absentmindedness battered little secondhand cars about the haunted, windblown heights of the ancient, secretive Hills. It was nothing to him either that he had brought them to an oasis of peace and beauty in an embattled age, where their town-cramped souls were already expanded into twice their former size, and their spirits had grown wings, and their nerves had unkinked themselves and relaxed into quiescence.

Be still, and know that I am God. . . . The words came suddenly out of nowhere, and Sabrina was surprised, because hers had not been a very religious upbringing. She wondered where she had first heard or read them—Psalms, she decided vaguely—wondered if Hilary had a Bible—idly pursued a faint recollection of one on the bottom shelf by the window—wondered how you went about it to find any certain half dozen words in the Bible—and fell to speculating on how much more important and beautiful the churches seemed in the country than in London. Perhaps it was because country people had more time to think things out quietly, as she was beginning to do, and to observe the loveliness of the world as God had left it, before cities were invented by man. Certainly one had a deep sense of gratitude to Somebody on a day like this, she reflected; one wanted to give thanks for just being born, for the golden warmth of the sun, for the color and fragrance of a garden, for red strawberries in a crystal bowl. *Be still, and know that I am God. . . .*

Just as the little procession of Mrs. Pilton with the tea-pot and silver urn on a tray, followed by Jennie with a plate of thin bread-and-butter left the house and started across the lawn, an open green four-seater with a solitary man at its wheel turned in at the gate and swept noisily along the drive to the steps, where it drew up with a flourish.

Sabrina's heart turned clean over. Here was the dream coming true. He had arrived. And there would be tea on the lawn just as she had always planned it, and perhaps a chance to get really acquainted with him, since Father was away at Maesbury for the whole day. . . .

"Who on earth can that be?" muttered Aunt Effie, dumping her basket and shears behind Sabrina's chair and pulling off the disreputable gloves she wore to garden in. "Just at tea-time, too, and with your father away for the afternoon. Be quiet, Bella, it isn't burglars anyway, in broad daylight! We shall have to offer him tea, I suppose. Tell Jennie to bring another cup, Sabrina, while I go and see who it is. He might have the wrong house— Don't be such a noisy girl, Bella, it's not polite!"

Preceded by the fat, yapping little dog, Aunt Effie crossed the grass towards the car. Sabrina had got out of her chair and stood watching, a thumping in her chest— the door on the near side of the car was opening— "Bring another cup, please, Jennie"—"Yes, miss"—and now he was coming towards her with Aunt Effie beside him and Bella bouncing and barking in front. . . .

Sabrina as she faced them realized that her knees were shaking and her hands were icy paws. He had taken off his hat now and carried it in his hand, uncovering non-descript blondish hair well flattened down on a roundish head above a big neck. The collar of his blue shirt was a bit too tight. His fair, soft skin had sunburned a bright pink. Expensive tailoring could not disguise the unyouthful bulkiness of his body in gray flannels. But this was never Hilary. . . .

"—well, yes, I could do with a spot of tea." His voice could be heard now, with its flat Mayfair note. "I had rather a scratch lunch in Town soon after twelve."

"You've driven all the way down from London since lunch time?" cried Aunt Effie, suitably impressed.

"Oh, rath-er! The old bus will touch eighty, you know, without turnin' a hair." Very off-hand about it.

No, no, not Hilary—please God, don't let Hilary be like this. . . .

"Well, we're very glad to have you join us at tea," Aunt Effie was saying cordially. "Do be quiet, Bella! Especially as Sabrina and I are all alone this afternoon and—. This is my niece Sabrina. This is Mr. Shenstone, dear."

"How do you do?" said Sabrina faintly. Not *my* Mr. Shenstone—not *Hilary*. . . .

"How d'ya do?" said the visitor, and his pale eyes rested a moment without interest on the white-faced girl who had risen to greet him, before they went on to the tea-table. "Good afternoon, Mrs. Pilton, still turning out those marvelous tea-cakes, I see! I suppose I shall make a pig of myself, as usual!"

"This is Master Hilary's favorite cake, sir—the one without currants. If you'd warned me you were coming, I could have made the other kind."

Relief surged through Sabrina. This was George! But of course it was George, she had known all the time it could never, never be Hilary, who liked his cakes plain. . . .

"Yes—as a matter of fact," said George, and his florid face clouded over, "—as a matter of fact, I've got rather bad news about my brother."

"I'm sorry to hear that, sir."

"B-bad news?" stammered Aunt Effie, with a glance at Sabrina who was staring at him dumbly and holding to the back of a chair.

"He was killed out in India, a few days ago."

"I'm very sorry, sir—"

"It came as a bit of a shock, though we hadn't heard from him for some time, and my mother had begun to be anxious. We thought—that is, we thought I had better come down here and see about his things, you know. The room can be cleared now, that is, so that you can have the use of it."

"Oh, but we don't need it, really—!" protested Aunt Effie automatically.

"My mother is still a bit upset, or she would have

come down herself," George explained. "I told her Mrs. Pilton and I could manage. Not a very pleasant job for her, you know—"

"Yes, of course—I mean—but you really must sit down comfortably and have some tea first, now that it's here," groped Aunt Effie.

"Thanks. I am a bit parched after the drive," he admitted, and his eyes were drawn back greedily to the tempting tea-table.

"Mrs. Pilton will go up to the room with you later on, and help you to—to do whatever is necessary, I'm sure," Aunt Effie assured him kindly.

"Yes, as I remember it he buzzed off to Town in something of a hurry, and then ordered the room to be locked up. Very cagey about his things, always—I used to tell him it looked like a guilty conscience to me—" The old jest lay unhappily on a silence.

Mrs. Pilton turned and went away across the grass, her footsteps making no sound, her face as inscrutable as ever. It was no shock to her to hear that Hilary, proxy-child of her barren heart, was dead. For several days, now, she had been schooling herself to the knowledge, so mysteriously come by in the Mendip dusk, that the strong, slender body she had watched emerge from childhood was in a rocky grave somewhere on the Frontier. Her anxiety now was all for the eager, restless spirit of him that had come home, and for the girl-child Sabrina who was somehow involved in his unfinished destiny. She was thinking as she reached the kitchen doorway and met Jennie returning with the extra cup, that it was a great pity that the news of his death had had to come like that to Sabrina, who had adopted him as a friend. She was wondering if it would frighten the child to know, as she herself knew, that he was here, in the house—but how could one speak of such a thing anyway, out loud, one could be burned as a witch in the old days for such an utterance. She wished that there was anything one could do or say to comfort Sabrina in this new loneliness. . . .

"Do sit down, Mr. Shenstone," Aunt Effie urged him helplessly, herself collapsing into the chair nearest the tea-pot. "Sabrina, darling, you'll feel better when you've had a cup of tea—"

"Please, Auntie, will you excuse me—" gasped Sabrina, and George noticed that the kid really was looking ill.

"But I'm just going to pour out, and here's Jennie with the extra cup, and see, there's such a lovely cake—" Aunt Effie was gazing up at her anxiously, the tea-pot poised.

"I—really don't want any tea—" Sabrina walked away blindly towards the house, praying not to cry before she reached it, breaking into a stumbling run when she had got as far as the drive.

"Oh, dear, perhaps if I could have broken it to her somehow—" said Aunt Effie, looking after her. "I'm afraid I must explain, Mr. Shenstone, that my niece has —has formed a childish attachment. She found her way into your brother's room without my knowing, and begged to be allowed to read the books he had there. Mrs. Pilton thought your mother wouldn't mind, so long as nothing was disturbed—"

"No, no, of course not—but what a rum idea," said George, looking bewildered.

"She is a strange child. I really don't understand her very well, I'm afraid. You see, she—she feels that she has become *personally* acquainted with the man whose books she has been reading, and—while of course I don't at *all* approve, I haven't been able to think of any way to put a stop to it, and so perhaps the news of your brother's death *was* a little sudden, and—"

"Oh, I say, I had no idea—"

"No, of course you hadn't, how could you? Please believe I am not blaming you. It is a thing she must learn to adjust herself to, and—"

"In those circumstances," began George, feeling his way among baffling female intricacies, "perhaps you would rather—I mean, I only came down to destroy any of his papers he might have left about, and—dispose of his clothes, and—things like that. Needn't make any difference in the room itself, really, she could go on using the books, I mean, and—"

"If you don't mind," interrupted Aunt Effie desperately, "I think it might be better if the room were definitely closed now."

"I think I see what you mean," said George, blinking.

"You see, now we have an excuse. You could say that your mother would like the room to be kept locked, for—

for sentimental reasons. I'm sure it would be—healthier, for Sabrina."

"Yes, of course—no doubt it would," he agreed thoughtfully.

"But I'm forgetting the tea!" cried Aunt Effie, leaping at it. "Do you take milk, Mr. Shenstone?"

"Milk and two lumps, please." There was a long and awkward silence. "Thank you," he said, accepting the cup, and promptly scalded himself in his embarrassment.

"I'm sure I don't know why we try to hold to India these days, it costs so many lives," said Aunt Effie nervously, preparing her own cup. "Still, your mother must be very proud of him—lie down, Bella, you'll get your tea later—though of course that's very poor comfort to her *yet*. Was your brother a soldier?"

"No, not exactly," said George, helping himself to bread-and-butter from the plate she offered. "He did odd jobs for the Home Office, you know. Something like this was bound to happen sooner or later."

"I see," said Aunt Effie rather blankly. There was a callousness in George's appetite for tea and bread-and-butter which she found rather appalling. She supposed the brothers hadn't seen each other for some time—and of course there had been several days for George's first grief to subside—and of course men never showed their real feelings, anyway. But after all, thought Aunt Effie, your own brother, whom you had known as a little boy—. Aunt Effie was sure that if she had had a sister who was killed—. *Men*, thought Aunt Effie hopelessly, and passed the bread-and-butter again.

"Thank you," said George. "You know, it's dashed queer to find something going on about his room down here too, because—. Well, I mean, you haven't noticed anything, have you?"

"Noticed anything?" she repeated, at sea.

"Yes, anything—unusual, about the room, I mean."

"Well, I can't keep Sabrina out of it," Aunt Effie admitted cautiously. "It's as though she was bewitched by the place. I've never known her to deliberately defy my wishes before. And for no *reason*, except that she likes to sit up there and read!"

"Well, then," said George, looking relieved, "I suppose there's nothing in it really, or she wouldn't want to—. I mean, she'd have noticed something herself, what?"

"Noticed something?" asked Aunt Effie, with a vague uneasiness. "What would she notice?"

"Well, it's hard to say, exactly. Only—there's a full-fledged ghost story going round about his room at the Club, and I naturally wondered—. But a kid like that would be scared off sooner than anybody, I should think."

Aunt Effie was staring at him in consternation.

"You mean the room might be *haunted?*" she whispered.

"Well, no, it's not the sort of thing one can easily swallow, especially about one's own brother," said George reasonably. "Perhaps I shouldn't have mentioned it at all, but just for a moment, when I heard his room was giving trouble here at home as well, I did wonder—. But if as you say the kid likes to sit there alone, there certainly can't be anything of that sort going on."

"No, I suppose not," agreed Aunt Effie doubtfully.

"Er—about that kitchen flue," said George, with a business-like clearing of his throat. "All right now?"

"Yes, thank you, the man came and cleaned it out. You should have *seen* what came down! And we're quite certain that one of the gas-pipes is leaking somewhere, and of course that's very dangerous, isn't it? I was going to write your mother, but now that you're here—"

"Oh. Well, I suppose we'd better have a man down from the company to look round a bit. I wouldn't be alarmed, though, if I were you. I mean, it won't blow up or anything. I'll stop at the office in Wells on my way back to Town. Anything else?"

"Well, if you remember, I did write about that tree at the end of the drive."

"Oh, yes, er—I was coming to that."

"It's dreadfully in the way, if you want to turn left going out of the gate. You see, I'm the chauffeur in this family, and—"

George set down an empty cup.

"Yes, now, I've been thinking," he began persuasively, "there's a first class gag with a large mirror—thank you, I *would* like another, if you don't mind—they put up a large mirror, y'know, facing the entrance of the drive from across the road—"

XII

SABRINA, flung face down across Hilary's bed, drained dry of tears and spent with sobbing, heard them—too late—coming up the stairs. Hilary, who was hanging over her in an agony of helplessness—"*But I'm here, my darling—I'm quite safe, I've come back to you, can't you understand?*"—retreated to the far corner by the chest of drawers to watch whatever form of desecration George would choose to visit upon his brother's property.

He had been sitting by the window when George drove up, and so had witnessed the brief tableau under the tree, and Sabrina's stumbling escape to the house. Her first headlong dash for sanctuary had carried her blindly past her own bedroom door and up the second flight of stairs to him. But so far it was beyond his power to penetrate her grief with any sense of his usual invisible presence. Just as she was quieting, limp and receptive, just as he hoped to reach her once more with some form of comfort, George and Aunt Effie entered, followed by Mrs. Pilton carrying a pile of folded dust-sheets.

Sabrina sat up on the bed and looked at them bleakly, making no move to go.

"Oh, there you are, darling," Aunt Effie began, too

brightly. "We were just saying downstairs, you mustn't take this too hard. Because after all, as Mr. Shenstone has very sensibly pointed out, it isn't as though you had ever actually *met* his brother, is it!"

"No, Auntie," said Sabrina, sitting still, her eyes on the floor.

"Mr. Shenstone's mother feels that if we don't *need* the room, which of course we don't, she would like to keep it closed for a while. I was just saying to Mr. Shenstone that I was sure you would agree out of respect for his mother's sorrow, not to come here any more."

"Yes, Auntie."

"So Mrs. Pilton is going to put out the dust-sheets, just as they always used to do when he was coming back, you know, and draw the curtains, just to keep the sun from the carpet, and—"

While Aunt Effie prattled on, Sabrina's eyes sought the housekeeper's in a look of sheer despair. Without seeming to avoid that appealing glance, but equally without responding to it, Mrs. Pilton bent to shroud a chair with swift, competent movements. Her dark, secretive face was set in its habitual calm, she was as self-contained and remote as a deaf-mute. It might have been a stranger who had died, thought Sabrina, with a brief moment of wonder at the woman's inhuman composure, instead of a man whose favorite cake she still baked for tea.

And George—her eyes went back heavily to Hilary's brother, who obviously ate too much, and who hadn't even the decency to wear a black band on his sleeve.

George was at the defenseless desk. Efficiently his thick hands went through the blotter and the drawers down the left side, tearing the written sheets of personal letters across and across as he came to them.

"No form of will, I suppose," he was saying, "unless it's at his banker's. Not that the poor beggar had much to leave, I fancy. You don't get much pay in his line, they only want your life, that's all! Good job he never married. Here's a file of some kind, I'd better take it back to Town with me, it seems to be mostly bills and that. I suppose some of them will have to be paid, nobody knows anything about his affairs—"

"You'll get the shock of your life, old boy, when you find you've got nothing there but receipts," said Hilary from the corner. *"I'm paid up, thank you very much, and hoping you are the same!"*

"Perhaps your little niece would like to have some form of keepsake," George suggested, considering Sabrina twelve years old at most, and only meaning to be kind. "Before the room is closed, I mean."

"Oh, shut up, George, for heaven's sake!" Hilary implored him, but Aunt Effie caught at the idea eagerly.

"Well, I'm sure that's very generous of you, Mr. Shenstone, if you think your mother wouldn't mind—"

"No, no, rather not, the mater would be only too willing—. Perhaps one of these book-ends now—he thought a lot of those, I happen to know—brought them back from Egypt one time—I believe they're supposed to be rather good. Or perhaps she'd like to have his fountain pen. That would be useful, wouldn't it—"

"No, thank you," gulped Sabrina, fighting off waves of sickness with clenched hands. "I wouldn't like to take anything—away—"

"Well, just as you feel about it, my dear," said George heartily. "He was a tidy old blighter, wasn't he! Not much to do here after all! Oh, yes, his clothes. Mother said he took almost nothing with him that day, and the village people might as well have whatever's here." He went to set the carved leaves of the wardrobe ajar. "I'll leave all that to you, Mrs. Pilton, you'll know where they'll come in handiest—"

"No, no, you shan't touch his things!" cried Sabrina, and sprang up to snatch the wardrobe door out of his hand and slammed it shut and set her back against it protectively. "Haven't you any feeling—haven't you any common decency, to give his things away to the first village lout who happens to be the same size?"

"Sabrina!" gasped Aunt Effie, shocked to the core.

"Well, I—I see what you mean, of course," said George uncomfortably, taken quite aback by so much vehemence in so negligible a creature as this thin girl had seemed to be. "But mother said the moth might be in them. We thought it would be rather a pity to waste things that some poor bloke might have a real use for—"

"You've no right to give away his things," insisted Sabrina, and still flattened against the wardrobe she began to cry again in a weak, spent way, bent over sidewise as though she had a broken wing, thought George, watching her helplessly and wondering if the aunt couldn't do something to stop her making all this row. "They belong here—they belong to him—please leave the room alone—please go away—"

"Sabrina, I think you had better come downstairs now," Aunt Effie interposed futilely. "Mr. Shenstone will hardly know what to think of you—" Already her mind was composing one of the periodic domestic inventories which drove her brother out onto the Hills or into the museum at Wells until whatever it was had been dealt with in her own muddleheaded way. That any niece of mine should be so tactless in a situation which was already difficult enough, she would say—and it wasn't as though she had the slightest right to be in the room at all, much less to interfere with Mr. Shenstone when he was only carrying out his mother's wishes. . . .

"Mrs. Pilton," cried Sabrina, clinging to the wardrobe door, "promise you won't take his things away! Promise you'll leave his clothes—"

The housekeeper straightened from swathing the bed in white, and her eyes met Sabrina's across it, and then went on to Aunt Effie's dismayed face, and came at last to George, who was wishing he had brought his mother along to tell him what to do.

"I think, sir, that at least for the time being—"

"Very well, Mrs. Pilton, I leave it entirely to you," he agreed hastily.

"Thank you, sir."

"Now, Sabrina, you're overwrought and hysterical." Aunt Effie laid an urgent arm about her. "I want you to come along to your room and lie down quietly till dinner time."

But Sabrina broke away from her to catch desperately at George's sleeve.

"Oh, please don't shut me out of here again!" she begged. "The room is alive, can't you feel that? You've no right to put it in a shroud! Besides, your brother likes me to be here, I know he does, and surely if you explained to your mother—"

"Sabrina, be quiet!" cried Aunt Effie, and in desperation caught her arm and began to pull her towards the door. "You are putting Mr. Shenstone in a most uncomfortable situation. You must understand that his mother has a—a sentiment about the room now, and it's very wrong of you to insist on intruding! I can't *think* what's got into you about this room—!" She broke off with a little gasp. Over Sabrina's shoulder, her eyes met George Shenstone's slightly strained and protruding gaze. The same thought was in both their minds. A room at the club—a room here at Nuns Farthing—both of them Hilary's—and both of them queer.

"*Cut it short, George, and clear out of here,*" said Hilary from the background. "*You've done enough damage for one day.*"

"I'm sorry to put you to all this trouble," said George, for the sake of saying something commonplace and normal in the midst of all this hysteria. "I shan't be long now, I'll just draw the curtains—" He turned away from Aunt Effie's startled eyes without, he hoped, allowing her to perceive that he was thinking the same thing she was. Much better if he hadn't mentioned that business at the club. . . . He was conscious of an overpowering desire to be on the way back to Town again, pelting along in the noisy green Bentley—yes, with a drink in sight somewhere on the way.

"You'll find me in the south drawing-room," said Aunt Effie. "I'll just tuck up this silly girl under an eiderdown, and wait for you downstairs, in case there's anything else—"

Thwarted, rebellious, convinced of some deliberate conspiracy against herself, and against Hilary if it came to that, Sabrina allowed Aunt Effie to lead her away towards her own room. She glanced back from the top of the stairs, and saw George reaching to draw the curtains across the sunny window by the desk, and noticed how his coat pulled in ugly straining wrinkles across his ugly fat back. . . .

XIII

FOR the next few days she went about much the same as usual, a little too quiet, with shadows under her eyes. The time she had habitually spent in Hilary's room she spent in her own, reading her own books; or sometimes just sitting on her window seat looking down into the garden. But she did not cry any more, and Aunt Effie assured herself hopefully that it was only a phase, and that it was passing.

Meanwhile, somewhat belatedly, Aunt Effie arranged for the adoption of a kitten out of a family in the barn at the farm where the eggs came from. Muffin was his name, and he was very small and black and intelligent, and selected Sabrina at once as his sole owner in all the household.

At last on a day when loneliness enveloped her like a fog, as night came on she went and sat on the top step of the second flight of stairs, her arms clasped round her knees and her head resting on them. Hilary, imprisoned behind the locked door, had heard her coming up the stairs, and guessed how she sat there on the steps, as near to him as she could get, pathetically alone.

As the sun went down he heard her being called to

dinner, and knew that she went unwillingly, drooping, with reluctant feet. Fuming at his own helplessness to put things right for her, presumably by knocking Aunt Effie's head against the wall till she saw reason, Hilary paced the floor restlessly, while shadows crept in towards the house from the drowsing garden, and panels of light spread outwards across the grass from uncurtained windows on the ground floor, for the night was sultry and everything stood open to catch a breeze.

Thunder muttered among the hills, and lightning glimmered sullenly now and then, but the storm held off and night fell with an almost audible thud, engulfing everything in thick darkness without a leaf stirring. Headache weather, he thought, standing idly at a window in his unlighted room after deciding there was no possible way down the outside wall short of climbing on the sill and jumping into space—and somehow he didn't feel quite up to that, not tonight. Anyway, even if he got out, Sabrina still couldn't get in, unless he contrived to find and steal the key, which was bound to make talk. Even if he unlocked the door for her, how would she know. . . .

The poor kid will go off to bed early with a book if she's wise, he thought. I wonder what she's reading now, all by herself. Well, make up your mind, Shenstone, what are we going to do about this, it can't go on indefinitely. . . .

But there must be some way, he argued irritably. If I could get at Pilton—. He went close to the locked door and listened. No sound. But I oughtn't to mind locks any more, he reminded himself. It ought to be possible to . . . No one was looking . . . At least it was worth a try. . . .

Deliberately he walked up against, into, and through the closed door, arriving on the other side with an expression of pleased surprise. But of course! How simple! And why not? It was all in learning how! Obviously the possibilities of a disembodied state were limitless and only needed to be explored.

There was a dim light over the lower staircase at the end of the hall, and Sabrina's door midway was closed. He rested a thoughtful glance on it as he passed by, toward the stairs. No. Better not. Better try Pilton.

He went on along the passage and started down the stairs on the way to the kitchen via the lower hall and the dining-room. Inevitably as he reached the landing Aunt Effie came into view at the bottom, with Bella in attendance.

At first he thought he would try to slip past, but as Aunt Effie's foot touched the bottom step Bella gave tongue hysterically. Caught only a few steps from the bottom, he flattened himself against the wainscoting and waited for the noise to subside.

"Bella, what *is* the matter with you? What makes you go off like that? Do be quiet, you'll disturb Uncle Alan again! Come along, now, don't be such a silly girl—"

Aunt Effie went up two or three more steps and paused to look back at the shrieking little dog, whose sharp muzzle was pointed unmistakably at the wainscoting just beside her. Helplessly Aunt Effie stared at the polished wood from ceiling to steps, while Hilary stood motionless and smiling directly in her line of vision. Experimentally then she put out her hand and touched the paneling behind him. And as she did so Aunt Effie felt a little queer, as though she had touched something—unaccustomed. She backed away from the wall and stood against the bannister, looking first at the wall in front of her and then at Bella, stiff-legged and pointing on the carpet below.

With a sudden spasm of panic, Aunt Effie scurried down the steps, scooped up the distraught Bella from the hall floor, and ran into the drawing-room and closed the door hard. And then, a few moments later she opened it again very cautiously, and looked out.

Just as she did so, Hilary was passing through the hall towards the dining-room, intent on his desire somehow to implant in Mrs. Pilton's receptive mind the idea that Sabrina must be allowed to come and go in his room as she chose. The hall was floored with stone, and the carpet left off a few feet on the near side of the dining-room threshold. The dining-room door, though unlatched, stood only half open. Aunt Effie, peering out from the drawing-room, heard footsteps leave the carpet and cross the stone floor, and saw the heavy dining-room door pushed back as by a hasty hand.

Aunt Effie felt a little faint.

That was bad, thought Hilary, reaching the dark sanctuary of the dining-room with relief. I oughtn't to upset

Aunt Effie, I'm unpopular enough as it is, on account of the room itself, without giving Bella fits on the stairs again. Perhaps I shouldn't have come down here at all. What conceivable good can it do. . . .

He paused in the pantry outside the swing door into the kitchen and listened. No voices. He pushed open the door an inch so that he could see into the lighted kitchen. Mrs. Pilton sat alone with her knitting. Recklessly he pushed the door further open, holding it back with his hand.

"*Mrs. Pilton,*" he said uncertainly, "*where's the key?*"

She looked up towards him silently, unstartled, her dark, secretive face never losing its matter-of-fact calm as she beheld the odd behavior of the swing door.

"*Give her the key, there's a lamb,*" he said.

Her eyes returned to the needles again, and the small, unhurried clicking resumed.

"You'd best go away now, Master Hilary," she remarked quietly. "Jennie only went out to get the linen off the bushes."

"*She'd stop grieving—I swear she would—if only you'd let her come and go as usual—*"

Jennie's quick footsteps in the scullery—Jennie's precipitate arrival in the doorway, her arms full of unfolded towels—

"Lor', what a night—black as your pocket! What's the matter, seen a ghost?"

Her eyes went to where the swing door still hung open, and as she looked it dropped silently back into place.

Jennie gave a small, surprised squeak above the armload of linen.

"Be quiet," said Mrs. Pilton sharply. "I didn't see anything."

Hilary faded away backwards into the nice dark dining-room. This wasn't doing anybody any good. Twice over he'd put his foot in it tonight. Better get back where he belonged. I'll be clanking chains and howling down the chimneys next, he thought. Well, anyway, I don't have to carry my head under my arm.

He retraced his steps cautiously through the hall and up the stairs. Once more his eyes rested thoughtfully on Sabrina's closed door. No. Not tonight. She mightn't like it, no matter how careful he was. Besides, one couldn't go barging into a girl's bedroom. . . . He went on up the second flight of stairs, and passed again without mishap through his own door.

After he had reached the upper passage, Aunt Effie emerged from the study on the ground floor, leading Father by the coat-sleeve and carrying Bella under one arm.

"It was there—on about the fourth step up," she whispered, and cleared her throat and went on quaveringly. "Bella saw It first—didn't you, darling? Well, I don't mean to say I exactly *saw* It myself, but—I'm sure I *touched* something!"

"Oh, come, now, Effie—"

"Well, then, I *didn't* touch anything—" said Aunt Effie, babbling with nerves, "—but It felt very queer!

So then I grabbed up Bella and ran into the living-room and looked out through a crack in the door—and It crossed the stone floor and went into the dining-room!"

"Well, we'll soon find out about that." Rather impatiently Father went into the dining-room too and switched on all the electric light. "There you are, Effie. No ghost in here. Put the dog down and see what happens."

Aunt Effie placed Bella on her feet just inside the door. The little dog ran about suspiciously for a moment with her ears cocked, and then returned, smiling and unperturbed, to Aunt Effie's side.

"There, you see?" said Father triumphantly. "Nothing here at all. And they've got a light on in the kitchen so no spook would go in there."

"But, Alan, I heard *footsteps*—"

"Nonsense. I was walking about in the study just before you came in, You heard me."

"F-footsteps on *stone*, Alan—"

"Now, Effie, I know that fellow Shenstone's visit upset you—talking about his dead brother, and locking up the room, and all that. But this is childish."

"I—I don't think I like this place after all. Alan, I'd like to leave."

"Leave? Leave what?"

"Leave this house," said Aunt Effie in a very small voice.

"That's impossible, I've taken a lease. Besides it's just

the thing for my work." Father began to recede towards the study again.

"*Alan!*" cried Aunt Effie desperately at his back.

"Yes—well?" He paused on the threshold.

"W-would you mind if I brought my needlework into the study tonight? I promise not to talk."

"Very well," he said patiently. "Does the dog have to come too?"

"Oh, Alan! It was Bella who *saw* It! She's ever so much more upset than I am!"

Father swallowed visibly.

"Come if you like," he said, and vanished within.

XIV

IT seemed to Sabrina a long time since she had first picked the lock of Hilary's room. Did his being dead now make all the difference between a room you could break into and a room you must leave locked? It was still difficult to think of him as dead. . . .

Slowly she groped her way to illumination. In the room he wasn't dead. Something of him was there, would always be there, waiting for her. Slowly the conviction grew that since George's visit—was it just her imagination?—since a little *before* George's visit Hilary had seemed nearer than during the spring, while he was still alive. It was as though Hilary dead was nearer. . . .

Wandering aimlessly along the border one morning, with Muffin under her arm and the warm July sun glinting on her fair hair, Sabrina began to see daylight in darkness. Why, then, it wasn't going to be so bad, after all. He was not entirely lost just because his thick-headed, thick-skinned brother drove up out of the blue to say he had been killed out in India. . . . But at that the old sick feeling began again, waves of chill and faintness. She fought it off, with clenched teeth and swimming eyes. To draw his curtains and put out dust-sheets and lock his door was nothing. Why, somewhere they must have buried a body that was his. But Hilary was here, at Nuns Farthing.

It was a boundlessly comforting idea. The game would be different now, for he was not going to arrive disconcertingly in a car—George had done that. Hilary would never come strolling across the lawn to her now, smiling and kind and terrifying—no, no, it's silly to cry, Hilary is just as much here as he ever was. There would never now be that agonizing moment just before he spoke for the first time, when you would pray for the sort of voice and the words you wanted to hear from him. Hilary would never say the wrong thing now, never fail to do the right thing. He would be always perfect, and safe, and inviolate, in her own heart—no, no, don't cry—Hilary will never go away now.

She had come to a standstill, gazing blindly at the dark red Richmond roses, which were a little heavy on their stems in the hot sun. The vases in Hilary's room. Had anyone thought to empty them? Mrs. Pilton, of course. There ought to be Richmond roses in Hilary's room today. . . .

"I don't think I care whether his mother likes it or not—and anyway, she needn't ever know," she said aloud, and Muffin purred against her side like a small warm dynamo. "We'll try the lock again this afternoon while Aunt Effie is at Wells. And we'll open the windows, and clear away the dust-sheets."

She could not have done without Muffin these days.

You could talk to him and he listened in a wise, receptive silence, without arguing.

So they saw Aunt Effie off in the car for Wells, with Bella on the seat beside her behaving like a lady, and then they burgled her dressing-table for more hairpins.

An hour later Sabrina was still on her knees outside Hilary's door, hot and discouraged. The lock would not give. Hilary was sitting on the top step, and Muffin lay on his back slapping at the air with soft, ineffectual paws and giggling as kittens can—for he was being deliciously tickled in the ribs by Hilary's invisible fingers, and loving it. The roses were wilting on the floor nearby.

"I suppose it was only an accident the first time," she sighed, pushing back her hair with a grimy hand. "I can never do it again. Muffin, you are an idiot, can't you suggest something?"

She stopped to listen guiltily, motionless, her head turned over her shoulder towards the stairs. Someone was coming up.

"*Ah,*" said Hilary with satisfaction. "*And about time too.*"

It was Mrs. Pilton. Sabrina, already flushed and rumpled with her failure at the lock, got still redder.

"I—I only wanted to air out the room a bit—" she began inadequately, and broke off, staring at the key in the housekeeper's outstretched hand. "Oh, Mrs. Pilton, it *is* nice of you!" She scrambled to her feet and took the key, and then, bending from the top step, put her arms round the woman's shoulders and kissed her cheek. "I can never thank you enough!"

"I may be wrong to let you have it," said Mrs. Pilton. "But he doesn't want you to be shut out."

"Oh—how do you know?" gasped Sabrina.

"It's hard to say, sometimes, how you know things." Mrs. Pilton turned back down the stairs. "I'll bring you up a cup of tea, if you like," she said.

"Thank you, that would be lovely!" Sabrina caught up Muffin and the drooping roses. "How things come about!" she marveled, as the key turned in the lock and the door swung back under her eager hand. "I've always imagined having tea with him, and now—"

The words died on her lips. For a moment she seemed about to cry out after Mrs. Pilton.

She herself had seen George at the window drawing the curtains while the dust-sheets glimmered eerily in the sudden twilight. But now sunshine flooded the window seat as usual and the shrouds had all been removed from the furniture and laid in a neatly folded pile in the corner.

"*Sorry*," said Hilary with real contrition. "*My first mistake.*"

He slipped past her into the room and surveyed it ruefully. If he had meant to devise a way to give evidence of his presence there he might have chosen just some such method as this—to restore with invisible hands the familiar, lived-in look of the room as they were both accustomed to it. But at the same time, it was a risk he would hardly have dared to take voluntarily, at least not yet, for fear of upsetting the delicate balance of their strange companionship, or of driving her away altogether. He did not like to think that she might be afraid of him. He had even contemplated some sort of revelation some day, if ever he felt secure enough. But this was too soon.

"*Please don't be frightened,*" he entreated her from the middle of the room. "*I shouldn't have moved the things. I wasn't thinking. But please don't let it put you off! Please, Sabrina—don't go away—*"

She came in very slowly and shut the door and stood against it. Her eyes were unusually wide and blue, and she was breathing fast as though she had run up the stairs. But she didn't look at all afraid.

"Hilary—" she whispered, holding tight to Muffin and the roses. "Where are you? I can't see you—I can't hear you—but I know you're here in this room. I've felt it before and—and now I know. And I'm glad. But how do I find you?"

"*You can't,*" he said, standing still by the mantelpiece, watching her. "*Not yet.*"

"Hilary—" (From where he stood half way across the room he could see the tiny pulse which beat in her thin throat.) "Hilary—who are you?"

"*I am the man you would have married, if things hadn't gone wrong,*" he told her simply, knowing it now himself with dizzying certainty.

But her eyes went past him and her next words took no notice of his.

"Can't you talk to me?" she begged, and it seemed the most reasonable request, with only the sentient air of that quiet room between them.

"*Evidently not yet,*" he said, and wondered why, when they were already so close.

"Hilary, I'm afraid!"

"*Not of me.*"

"I'm afraid of living—if you're dead. They'll always try to separate us."

"*They can't do that. Nothing can.*"

"Oh, why didn't you come home as I planned it! I'd have felt so safe with you, whatever happened!"

"*I meant to come. Something slipped—a matter of weeks—the timing went wrong.*"

"What did you say, Hilary—say it again—I nearly heard—"

"*Don't try, my darling. I'll wait.*"

"Wait for me, Hilary! Don't ever go away!"

"*I'll be here—always,*" he promised.

She glanced back suddenly at the door behind her. Mrs. Pilton, who had given her the key—he doesn't want you to be shut out. . . . Then Mrs. Pilton must know. . . .

Muffin squirmed in her tense hold, and yowled as a rose stem jabbed him, reminding her that the wilting flowers should go into water at once. She set the kitten down on the floor and carried the roses into the bathroom. She was neat and competent and quick as usual in all her movements, but she wore the rapt, remote look of a sleepwalker. Blindly she found the tooth-glass, filled it with water from the tap, and bundled the roses into it.

Her mind still refused to contemplate closely this thing which was happening to her. It was a thing so lucid and probable—so inevitable—and yet she knew with some far, dazed corner of her brain that Aunt Effie, for instance, would not think so. She told herself as it were parenthetically that Aunt Effie must never know about the dust-sheets. Mrs. Pilton might accept it, with her sublime composure. Mrs. Pilton was—well, perhaps used to him. But Aunt Effie would say she had been dreaming.

And at that word, Sabrina stood on the bathroom threshold with the cool glass of roses between her hands and that frantic pulse-beat in her throat, looking at the room again. It was not a dream, and the pile of dust-sheets was still there by the door. While on the hearthrug, his small tail carried high, Muffin was purring loudly and rubbing himself against friendly legs, about the reality of which he himself had obviously no doubts at all.

Something inside Sabrina turned clean over then, with a throbbing thrill which nearly choked her—and was still. It left her knees feeling like wet tissue paper, and in its wake came flooding a warm sweet languor of peaceful certainty. She drew in a long, uneven breath almost a sigh, and passed one unsteady hand, damp from the tilted glass, across her eyes, like a child which wakes suddenly in a bright light. Hilary. Muffin had found him. Hilary stood there on the hearthrug—at last.

"You've—come home," she said, and the knowledge

raced and tingled in her own astonished body, as though for that brief moment of realization he had held her in his arms.

"*And you're glad*," he reminded her gently, seeing almost with pity how the roses quivered in the glass she held, and how her eyelids betrayed her like a newly wakened child's. "*It's all right, my darling—I've been here for days—*"

A moment more she stood motionless, watching the empty air above the blissful kitten, unable to conjure up the faintest outline of what she knew must be there. Then with a reckless gasp of decision she started forward, one questing hand outstretched—

"*Don't*," said Hilary firmly, without moving. "*Don't try to touch me.*"

She halted a few feet short of him, and her hand retreated to fondle the drooping roses. She looked rather apologetic, and a little embarrassed. She was sure now that he stood there, within reach—as sure as though he had driven up in a car like George, for everyone to see. One must therefore behave as normally and sensibly one would behave in the circumstances, and not go clutching at him like a halfwit child. She was steadier now, quite suddenly. After all, she had known for days that he was here. . . .

"Lucky Muffin," she said, and went to place the glass of roses on the desk. "Such a clever kitten, to be able to see him!" She heard Mrs. Pilton coming up the stairs with the tea-tray, and spoke to her casually without looking round as the door opened. "I think the flowers will revive, don't you?"

Mrs. Pilton's eyes fell on the tooth-glass with disapproval.

"He's got a blue china bowl somewhere," she remarked. "He always kept his roses in that."

"Oh, of course—it's on the shelf in the bathroom!" Sabrina flew off to fetch it. "This is much better for them, it's smaller at the top," she said as she returned.

Mrs. Pilton was setting down the tea-tray on the smoking-table beside the chesterfield with an easy, habitual gesture. It was there that Hilary's tea-tray had always been laid.

"You oughtn't to go missing your tea the way you do when you come up here," she said, and her voice was as impersonal as ever on the kindly words. "Everybody needs a bit of something warm in the middle of the afternoon, I always think."

"Yes, I do get sort of empty," admitted Sabrina, raising her face from the roses with a radiant smile.

Like a bride, darted through the housekeeper's mind. Like a bride on her way from the altar. She's seen him, by the look of her eyes. No need to wonder how she'd take it. She knows. . . .

"There's a bit of extra milk there for Muffin, and a dish," the woman said unemotionally, and turned away towards the door.

"Mrs. Pilton." Sabrina had leaned both hands on the desk above the bowl of red roses—a casual, un-self-conscious pose which showed her fragile arms and the sweet turn of her head on its long throat. "Is it possible that anyone has been in the room since the day it was closed?"

"I don't see how. I had the key."

"I know. But when I came in just now the curtains were open, and the dust-sheets were folded up—over there." She pointed.

Mrs. Pilton had paused just inside the door, and their eyes met across the room, Sabrina's brilliantly blue and somehow triumphant—bridal. The housekeeper's usual hooded look, remote and unrevealing, slid away from that too dazzling gaze. She stooped and gathered up the dust-sheets competently.

"He always hates to see the place shrouded up like that," she said. "I'll put these away again."

The door closed behind her.

XV

THE days slipped by quietly into July, and at first Aunt Effie credited Sabrina's apparent contentment to the happy inspiration of producing Muffin at the psychological moment. Then gradually it dawned on her that Sabrina was using the room again, and that it must be with Mrs. Pilton's consent.

For a few more days Aunt Effie hoped she was wrong, pretended not to notice, put off bringing the matter up. One night, quite late, when Sabrina supposedly had gone to bed, Aunt Effie remembered that she had left her gardening shears and basket out in the dew at the edge of the border and ran out to fetch them in. As she returned to the house she saw a line of light between the curtains of the room at the top of the house, and she made up her mind to take a firm stand. If Sabrina was up there at this hour, reading . . .

She went into the house and climbed the stairs, Bella pattering at her heels. Sabrina's room was lighted behind a closed door, but Aunt Effie passed it by and came to the second flight. There Bella balked.

"Come along, pettie," said Aunt Effie over her shoulder, from the fourth step up.

"Woof!" said Bella in a mere whisper at the bottom.

"Come, Bella," Aunt Effie insisted, but Bella made odd small noises in her throat and stayed where she was.

Aunt Effie felt a little queer. The lights were certainly on, and so the door must have been unlocked. Gathering herself together, she went on up the stairs, laid her hand on the knob and opened the door.

"Sabrina?" she said uncertainly.

The brightly lighted room was empty.

Hilary had had time to lay down his book and retreat to the farthest corner by the chest of drawers when he heard her coming. He realized that to turn off the lights, too late, would only have given her the added fright of facing a dark room, and created an added mystery.

Aunt Effie gazed about her unhappily for a moment, and then found the master switch near the door and pressed it. She closed the door hastily and hastily descended the stairs to the passage, where Bella welcomed her as though she had returned from the North Pole.

For once oblivious of the little dog, Aunt Effie went to Sabrina's door, knocked, and put her head in. Sabrina was reading in bed, and turned a smiling, innocent face towards her visitor.

"Hello, Auntie," she said. "Going to bed now?"

Aunt Effie glanced behind her into the passage and then spoke in a lowered voice.

"Sabrina—when were you in that room last?"

With only an instant's hesitation, Sabrina told the truth.

"This afternoon."

"Before dark?"

"Yes, Auntie."

"But I have just found all the lights on up there," said Aunt Effie, and her eyes were round and scared, and sought reassurance.

With only an instant's hesitation, Sabrina tried to lie. "Oh, yes—I did run up for just a minute on my way to bed—to make sure I'd put my book back, I mean. I must have left them on then."

"Bella wouldn't go up there with me just now," said Aunt Effie, grave and nervous and not satisfied. "Not an inch beyond the bottom step. I thought she might be going off into one of her barking spells, but she only stood there, looking *queer*."

"Bella's fat and lazy," Sabrina hazarded unconvincingly, conscious that her heart was beating rather fast. "What made you think the lights were on up there?"

"I didn't *think* they were on, I *saw* them. I turned them off myself. I noticed light between the curtains when I went out for my scissors, and I thought it was you reading his books again—"

"Not guilty this time—but it's my fault all the same," she added quickly with compunction, for Aunt Effie looked badly shaken. She knew it would be useless to try to explain Hilary to Aunt Effie, who wasn't friends with him and therefore was bound to think he couldn't (or shouldn't) be there, or that she (Sabrina) was imagining things. It was very tiresome of him to have given himself away like that, and started Aunt Effie thinking. What a mercy she didn't know about the dust-sheets too! Looking at it from Aunt Effie's viewpoint, she could concede that it might be very disturbing to have someone round the house who moved things and left lights on and yet couldn't be seen. If it hadn't been Hilary, she might not have liked it herself, thought Sabrina, striving to be fair.

Aunt Effie came to the bed and kissed her perfunctorily.

"Good-night, dear. Don't read too late. Come, Bella—"

"Good-night, Auntie."

Aunt Effie went down to the living-room and found her needlework in its embroidered bag with wooden handles. Then she rang the bell, and settled herself in an armchair under a bridge-lamp.

It was Jennie who answered the bell.

"Please tell Mrs. Pilton I want to speak to her," said Aunt Effie, with hardly a glance up from her busy needle.

In a few minutes the housekeeper stood before her in the lamplight, composed and inscrutable as always. Aunt Effie found it even more awkward than she had anticipated.

"Did you give my niece the key to that room upstairs?" she began, rather obliquely.

"Yes, I did. I knew it was the only way to stop her fretting."

"But you knew it was against my wishes."

"I hoped you might overlook that if you saw a change for the better in her."

"I'm afraid I can't afford to overlook it. The day Mr. Shenstone was here and I learned—learned of his brother's death," pursued Aunt Effie with difficulty, "I decided that it would be better for the child—*healthier*—if she was not allowed to enter the room again."

"If I might say so, I think you're going the wrong way about it to try and force Miss Sabrina in this thing," said the housekeeper astonishingly, so that Aunt Effie glanced up at her over her spectacles, needle poised. "It will only drive her into herself."

"She's at such a trying age," sighed Aunt Effie, her assumed self-confidence ebbing visibly. "It's hard to know what to do."

"Then I'd say it was safer to let her alone. It won't do to make too much of it."

"But I don't feel it's *natural!*" cried Aunt Effie, and was uncomfortably aware of a brief flicker in the woman's eyes. "Do *you?*" she insisted, leaning forward in her eagerness for the answer.

"That's hard to say," Mrs. Pilton said cautiously. "It might be."

"Mrs. Pilton—have you ever felt there's something—well, something *strange* about this house lately?" Her taut nerves gave way under the housekeeper's habitual slowness to answer a question she did not like. "You *have* noticed something! So has Bella! So have I!"

"Most houses have something strange about them, one

way or another," was all Mrs. Pilton would say to that.

"Then you admit there *is* something! Do you know what it is?"

Again the answer was too long in coming.

"You must tell me," Aunt Effie implored. "Have you *seen* anything?"

"No."

"I know what you mean," she nodded. "It opens doors—and yet It isn't there! Bella and I met It on the stairs. Bella was terrified."

"It's nothing to be afraid of, I'm sure," said Mrs. Pilton, and it was almost as though she had smiled.

Aunt Effie stared at her anxiously, her needlework forgotten.

"But how do you know that? *What is It?*"

"It might be someone who once lived in the house—and has come home again," the woman replied simply, but Aunt Effie rose from her chair with a little cry of comprehension and horror.

"The one who was killed in India! His own brother said there was something queer about his room at the club. But this is awful!" cried Aunt Effie. "I must take her away at once!"

"It might be better just to let things take their course."

"You can't seriously stand there and tell me I should do nothing to save my niece from this—Thing?"

"There's no harm in him."

"What does It want, then?"

Again the woman's impregnable, self-possessed silence fell between them, and Aunt Effie shuddered.

"She goes and sits in that room—! Oh, no, it's too dreadful, I shall speak to my brother about it tonight. We'll have to leave here at once, even if it means breaking the lease, though I should think in the circumstances the family would hardly care to make an issue of it! I—I've never lived in a haunted house before!"

"You can't be sure of that, can you?" The housekeeper stooped and retrieved Aunt Effie's needlework from the floor. "Most old houses are haunted, one way or another."

"I—I must speak to my brother—"

"If I might say so," began Mrs. Pilton, and the quiet words were like a restraining hand on Aunt Effie's arm, "you ought to think twice before you try to take Miss Sabrina right out of the house. It might be dangerous to interfere."

"Dangerous to—!" That left Aunt Effie very nearly speechless. "I didn't mind very much when she began to make a—a friend of a man she would probably never meet," she floundered. "B-but now it's as though she had—fallen in love with some sort of—*ghost!* You should have told me about this sooner! You should have warned me!"

"I thought the best way would be to pretend we didn't notice anything at all."

"But that's impossible! It can't go on! Where would it lead to?"

"She might outgrow it. Or he might go away. In any case, it isn't a thing you can decide about."

"I have already decided!" said Aunt Effie obstinately. "We shall leave the house at once. I shall speak to her father. We shall take her back to London as soon as possible."

"I suppose you must do as you think best," said Mrs. Pilton drily, and turned away as though dismissed. "Good-night."

For a moment Aunt Effie stood looking at the door which had closed behind the housekeeper. Mrs. Pilton's tacit acceptance of what was to Aunt Effie a terrifying and unnatural situation hung like an echo in the room. Aunt Effie still could not quite believe her ears. It was bad enough to feel that the house was inhabited by something—unearthly. But that Sabrina should be determined to—to hobnob with the—the . . .

Aunt Effie marched with resolute footsteps across the hall and tapped on her brother's study door.

"Alan, I must speak to you."

He looked up at her over his spectacles, his pen poised hopefully. But he saw no reprieve in her face and resigned himself with a polite sigh.

"Yes, Effie—what is it now?"

She came in and sat down on the edge of the chair at the end of the desk, facing him, her hands pressed tight together in her lap.

"Alan—I've just had the fright of my life."

"Been seeing things again?" he inquired, with his untimely facetiousness.

"It's not funny, Alan. I've been talking to Mrs. Pilton. I was right about this house. We've got to leave at once. We've got to go back to London."

In spite of his habitual preoccupation, something of her urgency communicated itself to him. For the first time in many weeks she had fully half his attention.

"You mustn't listen to the locals round here," he began reprovingly. "They're an odd lot. They'll have you believing anything."

"Mrs. Pilton is a very—rational woman, in her way," she insisted, and it crossed his mind that for a person of somewhat limited education and intelligence his sister's choice of words was often inspired. "And she admitted to me only a few minutes ago that this house is—possessed."

"My dear Effie—" he began, bringing his mind down to it at last.

"You've got to listen to me, Alan. It's on account of Sabrina. It's not healthy for her."

"Nonsense. The child's looking very well."

"Alan, I'm worried about her. It's that room upstairs—the one that belonged to the brother who d-died. She's got into it again. Mrs. Pilton *gave* her the key!"

"Well, so long as the family don't know—and who's to tell them?—I can't see that it matters much."

Aunt Effie looked at him hopelessly. The task of explaining to him about the brightly lighted, empty room where Bella wouldn't go, and about her unnerving interview with the housekeeper, was beyond her. Men were obtuse, inconsiderate wretches who made bad jokes at the wrong times, and never saw what was happening under their own noses. Men never tried to understand anything. Men . . .

Quite unexpectedly, even to herself, Aunt Effie began to cry.

"Effie!" He was thoroughly horrified. "Effie, what in the world—I had no idea you were so upset! Here—take my handkerchief! Effie, old girl, you mustn't do this—!"

At last Aunt Effie blew her nose, and visibly braced herself.

"Alan, I want to go back to Town. Just as soon as possible."

"But—good heavens, we've just settled in!" All his sympathy took flight before what he could only regard as her persistent unreasonableness.

"We must go, Alan. For Sabrina's sake. We must get her away from that room. It's not right for her to become so—obsessed—with a dead man's things. It's—it's macabre! She might go mad!"

"*I* am the one," said Father, with exaggerated patience, "who will go mad. Must we go all the way back to London to separate Sabrina from this—so-called obsession? Or would some other house in the district do?"

"No, no, we must go right away, Alan! Right away back to London! And I think Sabrina had better go off to some nice school again for a while, to occupy her mind."

"But the last time we put her in a school you distinctly told me that that sort of thing was no good to her!"

"I know," she sighed. "It's so hard to know what to do. I can never be sure—" For a dreary moment she contemplated the perplexities of school circulars and advertisements, all of a confusing sameness, so that you made your choice blindly, like flipping a coin, and hoped for the best. "But after all, I do think a good strict school, with regular hours, and—and a lights-out bell, and—and outdoor games, and *discipline*—"

"How old is she?" he asked suddenly.

"Why, Alan! Your own daughter! She'll be eighteen in September, you know that as well as I do!"

"That's old for a school, isn't it? I might have her tutored for Girton, I suppose—"

"Yes, Girton might do—all those nice Cambridge boys," agreed Aunt Effie vaguely. "And then there was that Swiss school I told you about the last time we talked schools—the one that teaches them skiing, along with all the usual things."

"Well, I don't know, Effie—"

"I think perhaps the Swiss school would be better in the circumstances. She might be a little older than most of the pupils there, but she's always been too old for her age, and I'm sure she needs young companionship."

"The best way to get that is not to be the eldest of

a group," he remarked with astounding penetration. "Wasn't that place pretty expensive?"

"You said it was at the time, but this is a special case, Alan. I do think that to get her right away from England for a while—"

"Very well, I'll think about it." This was an old dodge, to end a discussion he had tired of. It seldom worked any more.

"But we must do something *at once*, Alan, there's no time to go on thinking about it! I've an idea that Swiss school's catalogue is upstairs in my desk—with pictures of the dormitories, and—yes, I'm sure I could lay my hand on it in no time—"

"Yes, all right, I'll look at it tomorrow, my dear—"

"Well, I could just run up to my room now and fetch it—"

"Tomorrow will do," he said. His attention had begun to wander back to the papers before him. He had no desire to see the catalogue, he had seen school catalogues before and they were all alike, with pictures of singularly unattractive young females in hideous uniforms with bulgy legs being hearty and ungraceful at netball or lacrosse—Sabrina's legs, he had noticed, did not bulge—pictures of aggressively plain and unnecessarily stalwart games mistresses gripping tennis racquets and grinning at the camera—pictures of bare, healthful dormitories which roused disquieting memories of his own far distant youth—and always a picture of the sanatorium, which gave him a chill just to look at it. So the poor little beggar was in for it again, was she? Well, that was what it was to be young, people did what was best for you. Skiing? She would break her neck. There ought to be something more peaceable, more restful, more halcyon, for the education of helpless virgins, than the things one saw in school catalogues. There ought to be— "What about a convent school?" he inquired out of the blue.

"We-ell, Alan—" Aunt Effie began doubtfully, trying to orient herself to a totally new idea.

"It sounds prettier," he explained, to her further bewilderment. "Chapel bells, and—embroidery work," he floundered.

"We-ell—" Aunt Effie repeated, rather dazed. "Of course there's always the religious question, Alan—" She paused significantly, and tried to catch his eye.

"The what? Oh, I see. Well, it was only a suggestion." He picked up his pen.

She made a desperate clutch at his mental coat-tails, dragging him back from oblivion.

"Then you think I'd better write to the Swiss school in the morning, Alan, and ask if they can take her?"

"Why, yes, I suppose so, if you think that's the best." His eyes were fastened to the printed page before him, his momentary concern for his daughter's always problematical happiness no longer existed. One left such things to women, after all.

"And a letter to Mrs. Shenstone, about giving up this lease," added Aunt Effie with satisfaction. "I'm sure if you knew everything, you'd agree with me that it is the only possible course—"

"Yes, yes, I've always trusted your judgment with regard to Sabrina," he assured her hastily, not wanting to hear everything just now.

"Thank you, Alan, I must say you're being very reasonable about it, and I know it's upsetting to you, but I've had rather an upsetting time myself—"

"Yes, I'm sure you have. I'm sure of it," he said soothingly.

"In fact, it would have been better, as it turns out, if we had never left London at all."

"There I can't agree with you," he said flatly. "This summer has been of inestimable value to my work. Inestimable."

"Oh. But, Alan, I do think we'd make a great mistake to stay out our lease here. I do think—"

"All right, Effie, you have your reasons, I know. Some other time—" His pen began to move again, across the paper.

"Well—good-night, Alan."

"Good-night, Effie."

XVI

SABRINA went down to breakfast the next morning in a very cautious state of mind, expecting to hear more about the lights in Hilary's room. But Father was behind the *Times*, as usual, and Aunt Effie seemed quite normal, remarking as she left the table that she had letters to write.

Sabrina went out into the garden to cut fresh flowers for Hilary's vases, and collected Muffin on her way upstairs. When she set him down inside the door he went at once to the window seat, jumped up on the sun-warmed cushions, rolled over to have his stomach rubbed, and began to purr loudly.

She watched him a moment, amused. His passion for Hilary's society endeared him to her. She envied him too, in his complete familiarity with the invisible presence which roused in herself no fear or strangeness. Without Muffin she would have been less sure of him, but the kitten obviously had no doubts at all about those friendly fingers in his ecstatic ribs.

"You can tell your friend Hilary to be more careful about these lights," she addressed Muffin severely, as she spread down yesterday's newspaper to lay the faded flowers on, and began to collect the vases to be changed. "Aunt Effie's mind was just settling down again, and now he's gone and got her *un*settled."

"I'm sorry about last night," said Hilary, very contrite. *"But I always did like lots of light, and now I don't even have to think about the bill!"*

"Precious Bella got a shock too, last night," Sabrina continued, returning from the bathroom with a vase full of fresh water in each hand. She placed them on the desk and began to fill one with roses and one with tall delphiniums which raised their pale blue spires well above her shining head.

"Have you any idea how pleasant it is for me to see you come into this room with your arms full of flowers?" he remarked irrelevantly.

"I can lie myself black in the face for him," she went on grumbling at Muffin, "but nothing will pacify Aunt Effie so long as Bella goes round having nerves and barking fits every so often. Bella isn't like you, she hates the sight of him."

"Tell Bella from me that it's entirely mutual," said Hilary, scratching Muffin's stomach on the window seat in the sun. *"I've known some extremely nice dogs in my time, but if ever I met a nasty-minded, ill-natured bitch, it's Bella!"*

"That's another thing," said Sabrina, along her own line of argument, and she paused with a long spray of delphinium in her hands. "What do you think, Muffin, does Bella see him?"

"You bet she does! We make faces at each other!" said Hilary.

"It seems hardly fair," she pondered, "when *I* can't see him."

"Ah, but I can see you!" he told her gallantly.

She was wrapping up the faded flowers neatly in the newspaper to take away downstairs. She put the newly filled vases back in their places, and took a dust-cloth out of the desk drawer.

"I must say he's a very tidy person to keep house for," she remarked. "No cigarette ash scattered about, no laundry to send away, no—"

She stood still, looking down at the seat of the arm-chair under the reading-light. A book lay there—a book she had never taken off the shelf. And the loose silk cushion was crumpled down into the corner against the arm.

"Wrong again," said Hilary uneasily. *"I'm getting careless. I meant to put it back."*

Once more there had come that paralyzing upheaval in her inside, fading into delicious lassitude and a sense of deep satisfaction and relief. Hilary. He was here, he was real, she had not imagined him, nothing mattered but that. Once more the impulse came to find him—make even surer of him—somehow to *see* him. She swung round towards the window seat—and then shyness again, a retreat into good manners. Behave sensibly, Sabrina, he can see you. Behave as though it was not unusual of him to leave things lying about. He has as good a right as anyone to put down a book wherever he chooses. Be tactful, Sabrina, and never let him know how your silly tummy acts when these things happen. Take it in your stride, Sabrina, he expects it of you. Take it the way Mrs. Pilton does, as though it was his own affair if he prefers not to be seen. . . .

Therefore, after that moment's pause, almost automatically she reached for the cushion and plumped it and set it back in place. Then, more slowly, she picked up the book he had been reading. It was black, with its title in gold letters—*True Ghost Stories.*

"We haven't read this one, Muffin," she remarked very casually, and only her eyes betrayed her, large and brightly blue, with languid lids. "I wonder if it's any good."

"*Well, I didn't find it very helpful,*" Hilary admitted, adoring her gameness, infinitely proud of her nervous take-up, pleased beyond all reason at how she took him in her stride and behaved superbly as though there was nothing unusual about him at all. "*I was hoping to learn something about the technique. The trouble is, they all take their haunting so seriously. It's too bad I haven't got some chains to rattle!*"

She searched the shelves briefly and returned the book to the empty space it had left. The one next to it was called *Historic British Ghosts.* Sabrina went on with her dusting, silent and very thoughtful.

The misplaced and forgotten book was the third tangible evidence of his actual presence in the room, without counting Muffin's behavior. And each time the same suffocating excitement pervaded her, which contained no element of fear. Each time too he seemed almost to emerge a little from invisibility. And meanwhile Muffin showed her where he sat. It seemed impossible now that if she turned suddenly to the window seat and asked him a question he should not answer. . . .

She approached the kitten, who lay on his side slapping happily with soft paws at elusive fingers to his left. She sat down on the other side of him, and the kitten grew quiet as the game stopped. Suddenly she laid her hand on Muffin's warm fur, and Hilary's fingers slid away from under hers with only an inch to spare.

"*No,*" he said quickly. "*You mustn't do things like that. I don't know what would happen if you touched me—so you mustn't do it.*"

He stood up and backed away from her to the chair beside the desk. It was a swivel, and as he sat down in it, facing her at the window, it shifted two inches to the left. Out of the tail of her eye she saw, and turned her head, and smiled at him in the desk chair, but said nothing more.

For a while she leaned on the sunny window sill, gazing down into the garden in their silent companionship. The kitten crept into her lap and went to sleep.

At last she stirred, with a long sigh.

"We'll have to go, Muffin," she said. "It's getting on for lunch time. And if we don't stay up here too long or too often, perhaps Aunt Effie won't mind so much."

She gathered up the sleepy kitten and the bundle of

faded flowers for the dustbin. At the door she looked back into the smiling, sun-drenched room, and waved a gay *au revoir* towards the desk.

The days went by uneventfully, and she kept house for him. No dust collected on the polished surfaces of his mahogany, and the cushions were always shaken up and set by the ears at the proper housemaid's angle. He found that if he persistently left the same book off the shelf she would read it. Or sometimes she had already read it, and would tell Muffin what she thought of it. Most of her conversation with Muffin included Hilary as well.

He had learned with a deep delight that it was not going to put her off to find something out of place in the room, and he even began to rummage out things she would never have found for herself that he wanted her to see, until gradually she could begin to piece together his life as she had once dreamed that he would reveal it to her if he returned.

Self-consciousness, prudence, his scrupulous care never to startle her, or some indefinable between-worlds etiquette which governed his actions made it impossible for him to come close to her, or to move things about when she was in the room. But often when she arrived at the door in the morning some new treasure had been exposed for her investigation.

The first of these exhibits had been involuntary. Regretting his lost *Junonia*, which must be in the useless parcel of his effects which Dalton would have dispatched from Peshawur to his family, he brought out from a lower shelf the tidy wooden boxes of his very select collection of butterflies and beetles. Each specimen was neatly pinned down with its label, which by his own key led to a little black notebook where the circumstances of its capture were recorded. It was a boyish scheme begun long ago for the entertainment of his suppositious old age. Somewhat ruefully he beheld them again, for his old age was a bit of a joke now.

Here was his *Parnassius*, an absolutely perfect specimen, taken in a flower-studded clearing on Mt. Huttu; and his first big yellow *Papilio*, on the way down to Narkanda; and the thrilling black *Heliconia* from Trinidad (and a long, hot chase that was, through vicious undergrowth, but worth it); and the ubiquitous *Danaida chrysippus*, this one from Khartum, beyond the waterworks.

He was still hovering over them lovingly when Sabrina came in, much earlier than usual, carrying pink ramblers with the dew still glinting on their petals, and a somewhat draggled kitten who had run through tall wet grass.

She stopped in the middle of the room, gazing at the unfamiliar boxes on the desk.

"Oh!" she gasped, and dumped down the roses and came to bend above the butterflies. "Oh, how lovely! Oh, what *are* they!"

"*The story of my life*," he told her, smiling, "*in butterflies' wings*."

"I never knew they were here! Look, Muffin—he's left

them out for us to see! And they've all got names, Muffin, don't you wish they could talk?"

"They can," he said, savoring her pleasure. *"I'll find my key for you."*

"There was a butterfly book somewhere—I've seen it on the shelf. Perhaps if we read it, we could learn something about them."

She carried the kitten to the shelves behind the chesterfield, and finally ran to earth the battered Kirby which had been at school with him, and returned with it in triumph to the desk.

"It's my own key you want," he said. And then, while he watched her becoming absorbed in the book, involved with its index and plate numbers, a new idea intruded itself.

Rather unwillingly he surveyed it from all sides. He didn't like it. It was dangerous and perhaps wholly unwise. But it would not go away. It was an idea born of the butterfly key he meant to give her: When he spoke she did not hear—but how if he wrote?

While he still contemplated with dismay this entirely unwelcome and disturbing question, Sabrina took a sheet of note-paper from the top drawer, found a pencil, and began to copy the *Papilio* page numbers from Kirby's index. She had only begun when Mrs. Pilton put her head round the door.

"Breakfast's going in," she said, and Sabrina thanked her and ran for the stairs.

Alone in the room, he eyed her pencil and paper very

thoughtfully indeed. There was plenty of blank space on that page for anything he cared to write there—any message to test this one last means of communication from him to her. He told himself that he dared not try—and yet he took the pencil in his hand. After all, the butterfly boxes had not upset her. . . .

He wondered what to write, and while he wondered the pencil had begun to move, below the page numbers she had copied. *You will find my butterfly key—a sort of diary—on the bottom shelf left of the mantelpiece.* No more. That would do. That was enough to begin with.

Muffin had been left behind in her flight, and as Hilary laid down the pencil he found the kitten watching him with its innocent blue gaze from the window seat.

"*Now we* have *done it*," he said unhappily, and in sudden panic he would have liked to erase the message entirely or destroy the paper on which he had written it. "*It's asking too much of her. Nobody's nerves could stand it. I was crazy to try.*"

Sabrina was back again remarkably soon, eager for the new game. She went straight to the desk and Kirby's index to resume her copying. Hilary watched her anxiously. Now for it.

Neatly her figures marched down the paper through his own written lines—and he saw with what he could only acknowledge as blinding relief and thanksgiving that to Sabrina's tranquil eyes no writing was there but her own.

When she came in the following day, his butterfly

diary awaited her on the desk. She opened it with reverent fingertips, incredulous of her good fortune. And so at last she encountered the man himself, first hand, running to meet him down the closely written pages, breathless with excitement. She followed him to Simla and the mountains beyond, to the Calcutta suburbs, to Cairo, Khartum, and most mysteriously to Trinidad, where a homesick padre, himself an ardent entomologist, had taken him to his own favorite collecting ground near the reservoir.

The reasons for Hilary's journeys to these far places were all left out, the duties he accomplished there were never mentioned. But Hilary himself emerged in essence from the pages—casual, humorous, leisurely, dramatically understated, infinitely lovable and sane; objecting to the prolonged death-struggles of the hardy *Parnassius* in a German missionary's killing-bottle when his own specimen was long since quiet after the usual expert pinch; objecting still more strongly to the prevalence of water-buffalo near a rich collecting field at Penang; objecting most strongly of all to a tiger-hunt which he had no wish to join; referring briefly to a place where two of his bearers had died; and even more tersely to some shooting which had occurred after the *Pyrameis* was taken, somewhere beyond Khyber. Afridis, Hindus, Arabs, and West Indians flashed past as she read. And always there was Hilary, equally ready for laughter or gunfire, and never approving of cyanide-bottles.

The little black notebook brought her a new world—

Hilary's world. It answered so many of her questions, it made him so near, so completely alive. It was a happiness beyond anything she had hoped for. It brought different books off the shelves, too, from the ones she had been accustomed to read; books about the places where he had been. India ceased to be Kipling a lifetime ago, and became Hilary only yesterday. Egypt was no longer just a pink place on the map, for Hilary had seen it, and brought back three butterflies. And Trinidad—one had hardly even heard of Trinidad, but Hilary had been there, and it was beautiful.

XVII

ONE rainy day she did not come, and towards tea time he got lonely. She must be somewhere in the house, he felt sure, on account of the weather. He went out and listened over the bannister but the house was very still—so still that the fine beat of rain against its window panes and the drip from its eaves could be heard where he stood. By leaning way out he could see the closed door of Sabrina's room, and a dim uneasiness pervaded him. Yesterday she had sneezed three times, and remarked philosophically to Muffin that she must be getting a cold. She might be ill. . . .

I suppose I'd better go down and snoop round a bit, he thought. Nobody ever tells me anything. He made quite sure that Bella was not in the upper passage and noiselessly descended his stairs, to hesitate outside Sabrina's door—suppose he knocked?—and then, recklessly, he walked into the door and came out on the other side. That's one useful thing I've learnt, anyhow, he congratulated himself.

But exactly as though he had opened the door and closed it again behind him, she looked up and knew he was there.

Wearing a soft pink dressing-gown and slippers, she was lying face down across the bed with her heels in the air and her chin in her hands, reading a book. And to his delight, she reacted instantly to her awareness of his presence by an instinctive clutch at the folds of the dressing-gown which fell open across her breast. For a moment, with parted lips and large eyes, one hand caught up against her throat, she stared towards the closed door.

His own reaction also was prompt and instinctive.

"*Sorry, darling, I never meant to startle you,*" he said, halting in his tracks. "*Shall I go away again?*"

Then, as Muffin bounded out into the middle of the room with his small tail erect and went to rub himself blissfully against those legs which were not invisible to him, she relaxed with a breath of laughter.

"Come in!" she said, with the mock formality of a children's tea-party. "I wasn't expecting you!"

Hilary stood grinning at her from near the door, Muffin purring round his feet. Her embarrassment, and then her self-possession, to the extent of clowning her welcome to him—this first glimpse of her dawning womanhood in dealing with a situation which he himself had created, enthralled him beyond anything he had dreamed.

"*You are an enchanting person,*" he said. "*And I think, in the circumstances, it is my privilege to stay.*"

She sat up, drawing her long silk legs under her on the bed.

"Ask your guest to sit down, Muffin, where are your

manners? Tea's coming up any minute. I only hope Bella won't come with it!"

"Oh, damn the dog!" Hilary sighed, and sat down in the armchair by the dressing-table. The room smelt faintly of eucalyptus, and she had a rolled-up ball of handkerchief in one hand. But it was certainly not a drippy cold, she didn't even look as though she had a cold, and—in fact, she looked as decorative in the pink dressing-gown as he had ever seen her. There was nothing to worry about, and he was glad he had come.

She thumped up the pillows and adjusted herself more decorously against them, with the book.

He saw with surprise that it was a five-years-old smart novel, probably one she had found in the room, perhaps one left there by Alice on a visit. It belonged to that mixed tribe which accumulate in guest-rooms. He was surprised too that it held her interest, and then perceived that she read it gravely and with no recognition of its mordant wittiness, and that to Sabrina in her endearing ignorance, it was Life.

At first he wanted to take it away from her, and then he reflected that she had to know the worst some day—if it was the worst. And he reflected too that in a way it was life, but not with a capital L. It had doubtless presented no revelations to Alice five years ago, for instance. Alice knew people like that. Well, let's face it, Alice herself belonged in a book like that. Alice and George. People who lived soft, and strove desperately to amuse themselves, chose and discarded partners in marriage almost as casually as though it was a bridge-game. Alice thought she loved George now, but—it was a rather sickening idea—how about five or six years from now? Alice would still be beautiful and would still want love. And George—let's face it—would be a dull lover and a duller husband. There wasn't much doubt that Alice was going to be bored, which would inevitably bore George. And when people like that became bored they were very likely to behave like almost any smart novel. George would find something young and bloodthirsty, and Alice in retaliation would find—what? He knew with a sudden gust of ghastly humor that first of all Alice would think of him, when George began to pall. And there, if he had come back alive, was the novel, and happening to himself. A close shave, he thought with the unerring, internal mirth he would never lose. A narrow squeak, if you like!

There was a companionable silence in the room, with the rain coming down outside.

He would have been less concerned at Sabrina's absorption in the book if he had realized what already lay behind her in the way of reading-matter. No one had ever censored the books she took from the library shelves in the London flat, or inspected those she got from Boots. She had always chosen at blithe random, by a title, the picture on a paper dust-cover, or the opening sentence of Chapter One. In this way she had covered a lot of ground, from George Eliot and the Brontës to Ethel M. Dell, from Hardy and Galsworthy to Wallace and Waugh. Fortunately a great deal of what she read had passed her by, and some of it she misinterpreted. Most of the rest of it was not reassuring.

For years, it seemed to her, she had read whatever she read in search of something to steer by, trying to find clues to the puzzle of living, hoping for enlightenment on matters she did not comprehend. It was all pretty useless, because new problems presented themselves faster than old ones got solved. She had a touching faith in the printed word. These people who wrote must know. These things must be so. Sometimes the prospect presented to her, of growing up and getting married or not getting married, of having children or not having children, of meeting men and women on equal terms, yes, just of living a life, oppressed her with such a terror of her own future that she lay awake in the dark in a hopeless funk, trying to pray without knowing what for.

She would watch people in buses and trains and restaurants with a kind of envious awe—people who seemed to know exactly what to say and do, people who lived competently as wives or mothers, responsible for the happiness of men they had married and children they had borne. I could never do it, she would decide despairingly—I wouldn't know how, I'd make an awful hash of it, I know I would. She watched the celluloid emotions of the cinema intently, trying to take it in, trying to see why x plus y equaled z, believing that these people were behaving with logic and acting on reason—and in consequence getting more bogged down than ever. The newspapers were full of murderings and suicides and wars.

One went to church and listened to sonorous men who professed to have the ear and to know the will of God. But where had it got them, after all?

Bewilderment had begun to smooth out since she came to Nuns Farthing. Here was a life one could cope with, one could go on forever like this, without daily misgivings about the future. Here, tomorrow would be like yesterday, and confidence unfolded like a flower in the sun. If it was possible to grow old like Mrs. Pilton—. But even here, one met uncertainty. For who and what was Mr. Pilton, and where was he, and how had Mrs. Pilton felt about him?

Men, and marriage, and children—and divorce. Aunt Effie had done without them all. And all Aunt Effie had now was Bella. And that wasn't right either. But Hilary would know the answers. Hilary could have explained what it was all about. And his very name meant laughter.

One wouldn't have been afraid to say anything, try anything, go anywhere, with Hilary. The thing now was to stay as close to him as possible, never to lose him. Here at Nuns Farthing, which was his home, one was safe. Perhaps that was why Father had been led to take the house in the first place, though he would never guess it—just to bring her safe to Hilary. So that now, when she read novels like this one, about people who had all married the wrong ones and were making themselves and everybody else perfectly miserable about it, she hadn't really got to worry because nothing of that sort could happen to her at Nuns Farthing. . . .

Mrs. Pilton herself brought up the tea-tray, with a fragrant buttered crumpet under a cover, and a generous slice of fresh cake with icing—not forgetting Muffin's tea-time thimbleful of milk in his own saucer. She glanced once round the quiet room and went away, closing the door softly behind her.

It was good China tea, and the aroma came to Hilary from Sabrina's cup as she poured. She did not speak to him again, perhaps because it seemed less natural to her out of the room upstairs, perhaps because his presence was less real to her in this one. He wished he could make her understand that he was not wholly confined to his own four walls except by prudence—and, of course, Bella.

Coming down here today had proved for him an illuminating adventure, expanding their horizons as it did. In the ordinary way he would be smoking a pipe in that armchair, after a cup of China tea and a crumpet. It interested him to notice today that instead of his former somewhat wistful reflection that he no longer needed such things as tobacco or tea, he was now receiving somehow from the sight of her tray the essence of his palate's one-time satisfaction. This set him pondering on what exactly he had retained of himself, and what he had left behind in a grave at Peshawur.

Sight, touch, hearing, and smell, and a memory of creature comforts—no, that was not quite right. Memory had very little to do with the satisfaction he drew from her appetizing tea-tray. It was as though, without the barriers of flesh and bone, sensation of all kinds reached him directly, acutely, in some distilled, immediate form, without hindrance. His mind was there, alive still, his spirit, once harassed by his body, was now free and quick and very aware. The pleasures he had enjoyed as a man all remained to him, accentuated, fined down—distilled.

All?

He looked at Sabrina, drinking her tea on the edge of the bed, reading her book over the brim of the cup, the pink satin folds of the dressing-gown framing her fragile throat—the small bones and delicate skin a clumsy man could bruise without knowing—and as he looked, he knew a surge of singing ecstasy which took him entirely by surprise, and opened up yet another vista before him.

He was in love with this little earthling, as surely and as deeply as though he had come back whole in his man's body and found her living here in his home—a love so strong and inevitable that even death had not robbed them of each other. A mistake had been made somewhere and one bullet got astray to drop him in the desert. Then reparation was swiftly made, too, as far as it could go. He had returned to Nuns Farthing, and slowly the distance between them was narrowing, by her instinctive trust and faith in him, by his increasing comprehension of himself as he now was.

Thus he must study to fulfill his fractured destiny, and to make what refuge he could for her from disillusionment and disaster; to stay with her, however he could, as long as she needed him; to make of himself a sort of guardian angel, always with her growing knowledge and consent. And some day, late or soon, it would be his privilege and his responsibility to see that she made the crossing safely and willingly and without fear, into his perpetual care.

Also, as he watched her drinking her tea, taking no further notice of him but the more content because he was there, he realized that to accept this state of affairs as he did, philosophically, was not just making the best of things. Rather, it was to appreciate a perfection of intimacy that two people bound by flesh and blood could never know.

XVIII

SABRINA'S cold did not materialize, and the next morning early she met the postman on her way down to breakfast. There was a copy of *Antiquity* for Father, and a large square envelope with a Swiss stamp for Aunt Effie.

Sabrina glanced at the latter in pardonable surprise and said, as she laid it beside Aunt Effie's plate—"Who's in Switzerland, Auntie?"

"Oh, Alan, it's come," said Aunt Effie, trying to catch his eye before *Antiquity* absorbed him.

"What's come?" said Father, slitting the wrapper.

"The letter from Switzerland. I told you I had written. This is the answer."

She tore it open with a glance at Sabrina, who was helping herself to kidneys and bacon at the sideboard hot-plate. There was a printed booklet on expensive shiny paper, and a rather long typed letter. Sabrina gave it a curious look as she sat down and began her breakfast in silence.

Finally—

"Alan, everything seems to be all right," Aunt Effie

announced with satisfaction. "Would you like to read the letter?"

"Not particularly," said Father from behind *Antiquity.*

"There's a list of things to be bought," said Aunt Effie.

"I don't doubt it," said Father.

"I think we'd better go up to Town by the first of the week."

Sabrina's sensitive nerve centers registered swift alarm.

"Why?" she said, and looked from one to the other. "Why go up to Town?"

"To buy clothes and things," Aunt Effie told her brightly—much too brightly. "You'll like that, won't you, dear?"

"I don't need any more clothes." Sabrina's heart had begun to beat thickly all by itself.

"But you will to go to Switzerland," said Aunt Effie, and Sabrina stared at her incredulously. "Oh, didn't I tell you?" Aunt Effie went on uneasily, knowing very well that she had not. "We thought it would be nice for you to have a few months at that lovely school near Geneva. It takes girls from twelve to twenty-two, so *that's* all right. It's time you brushed up your French, I'm sure, and besides they teach skiing, and then you're right at hand for all that wonderful music, and the mountain air must be very healthful after this heat—"

"What *are* you talking about?" gasped Sabrina. But somehow she knew already. She had been through this sort of thing before. "I'm not going to any school. I'm too old for school."

"Oh, no, not for this one! And besides—"

"I won't leave this house!" said Sabrina in a small, pinched voice, sitting very still. "I'm happy here—happier than I've ever been. I won't go."

"Darling, you mustn't talk like that, you know you'll do what Father and I think best for you. And besides, you don't know anything about it yet, how can you say whether you'll like it or not?"

"Father, will you please listen to me? You promised last time I needn't ever go to a school again. You promised!"

"Perhaps I was wrong to call this exactly a *school*," said Aunt Effie hastily. "It will be more like a nice holiday abroad with friends. I'm sure you'll make friends at once—"

"Father!" In desperation, Sabrina rose from her chair and snatched *Antiquity* out of his hands, so that he looked up at her in astonishment, over his spectacles. "Father, please don't send me away from here! Please say I haven't got to go!"

"Now, I don't want any hysteria," said Father firmly. "Your aunt has gone into the matter very thoroughly by now, I should imagine, and I think we had better not discuss it."

"But you can't just send me all the way to Switzerland without discussing it—"

"Now, darling, you're not to get over-excited," admonished Aunt Effie from the other side of the table. "Your father is willing to pay rather a large fee to give you this lovely surprise, and I must say it's not very grateful of you—"

"Of course I'm not grateful!" stormed Sabrina. "I love this house! I love the garden—I love the feel of things here! I can't go away now, this is *home*, the first real home I've ever had! Who on earth wants to go to the Continent anyway, they're all murdering each other over there!"

"Not in Switzerland," Aunt Effie objected feebly.

"Father, please say you'll give up this horrible idea and let me alone! I'm not ill, I'll study anything you like, I'll learn *Greek* if you'll only let me stay here, at home!"

Father rose, with his full teacup in one hand, and held out the other for *Antiquity*.

"When you have quite finished making a scene, Sabrina," he said coldly. "Thank you." He took the magazine out of her unresisting fingers and departed with dignity to his study, carrying his tea.

"There!" said Aunt Effie reproachfully. "Now he won't come out for hours, and I shall have to send in his luncheon on a tray, and that makes extra trouble in the kitchen. Sit down and eat your breakfast, Sabrina."

"Please, Auntie, I—"

"You haven't touched your plate. It's wasting good food."

With her eyes flooding helpless tears, Sabrina subsided

into her chair and began to choke down mouthfuls of cold bacon. She knew defeat when she met it. Father was on Aunt Effie's side, he always was, and Aunt Effie had made up her mind with the terrible obstinacy of the habitually indecisive. Nothing but the end of the world would save her now from that Swiss school which for some reason Aunt Effie had set her heart on. There was no one to appeal to, no arbiter whose power was greater than theirs who had sentenced her. She was done.

When at last she was able to get away from the table, she climbed the stairs to her own room and stood idly just inside the closed door, feeling beaten and sick and bewildered—and worst of all, trapped. The impulse to escape surged up in panic. How if, when they came to take her away, she could not be found? Her small square chin came up. Yes, of course—there was still time to disappear.

She seized a hat from the wardrobe, threw a coat over her arm, hurried to the dressing-table for her hand-bag. One's weekly allowance piled up at Nuns Farthing where there was no need to buy flowers or books or cakes for tea. She had accumulated something over two pounds. One could go a long way on two pounds. One could get a job as a waitress or something. . . .

On her way to the door she paused. There was something about luggage. You had to have luggage in order to get into a hotel. She turned back, pulled her dressing-case out of the wardrobe and flung overnight necessities into it. Then, with her coat draped over it the best she could, she tiptoed to the door and down the stairs. Aunt Effie would be in the kitchen now, doing the ordering. If one could get out of the grounds and catch the bus at the crossroads . . .

The cathedral clock was striking noon when she stepped down from the bus in the market place at Wells, trying to remember the way to the railway station, which she had never seen. Somewhere down to the left, she thought—one could ask at the Swan. . . . Another bus was loading, just where she stood. She raised her eyes to its sign. Glastonbury, and Street, it said. One day soon after they had arrived at Nuns Farthing she and Aunt Effie had driven over to Glastonbury and gone through the ruin with Aunt Effie's guide book, backed up by Sabrina's schoolgirl fondness for *The Idylls of the King.* It had been very peaceful and green and quiet, under the broken arches. Sanctuary. . . .

With a grinding of gears the Glastonbury bus began to get under way. Its rear door stood open, folded back. Sabrina ran after it, jumped recklessly for the step, and was saved by the young conductor, who caught her elbow roughly and pulled her up.

"Mustn't do that, miss," he said. "Gimme quite a turn, you did!"

"I'm sorry. You do go to Glastonbury—?"

"That's right, miss."

She dropped into a seat by the window, and sat clutching her ticket and staring out at the green countryside, the bag on the floor at her feet cramping them sidewise.

Very soon the Tor came into view on the left, goal of so many million pilgrimages since the beginning of Christian time in Britain—a tiny tower, remote and unreal, on an improbable, pudding-shaped hill rising out of the misty water meadows where Lake Villages used to be; Avalon, Isles of the Blest, where Merlin wrought and Arthur died. Nobody would think of looking for her at Glastonbury.

She had got away. But now, too late, she realized that she had left Hilary behind. What would he think, when she didn't come up to the room? He would go through the house then, searching for her, and finally he would hear from somebody that she had run away, and then he would worry. She should have let him know why she was going. Now there was no way to reach him at all. That was what panic did to you. You didn't think. You did the first mad, desperate thing that occurred to you, and then it was too late. But Hilary couldn't help her now, because she could not throw her arms round him and beg to stay with him at Nuns Farthing forever.

All the way to Glastonbury in the jerking, lumbering bus, she wondered about Hilary and what would become of him without her, and how she could ever get back to him now. In a daze she alighted in the little square of the old gray town and stood a moment holding her dressing-case and wondering what to do next. She turned instinctively under the arch of the gatehouse, paid sixpence at the turnstile, and went into the abbey ruin. Inevitably the sheer, heartcatching beauty of the place struck through her preoccupation, and brought her up short on the path, humbled and comforted at the same time by its ravished splendor.

Warm sunlight gilded the green aisles open to the sky, the exquisite broken arches cast short midday shadows on the grass. Here Joseph of Arimathea came, when he had buried Christ, and built a little homely church of thatch and reeds to house the Grail. Here St. Patrick taught the youthful St. Benignus, and St. Augustine came on a visit, bringing the black Benedictine habit. Here St. Dunstan spent his young days, and when his bones came back from Canterbury for burial, while the procession was yet a mile from the abbey the bells burst into a joyous peal of their own accord to welcome him home again. Here, in the new Norman church with its round stone arches, Henry II and his queen beheld with reverence the giant bones of Arthur and the golden hair of Guinevere, whose coffin had been placed not at the king's side but at his feet, as became an unfaithful wife and the sore conscience of her lover Lancelot. Here the wanton cruelty of the Dissolution fell on an honest, aged abbot, and after pillage and blasphemy the deserted abbey was left to crumble away, while cartloads of its wrought stone went to mend the cottages and pigstys of the peasantry.

All this it had survived, and now it was in good hands again, at peace, protected, dreaming in the sun, all passion spent, and still the holiest earth in Britain. And to it came Sabrina, embattled and afraid, but drawing up comfort and surcease through the soles of her small brogans. She found a low bank at the far end, and sat down there on her coat, her dressing-case beside her, and went on thinking about Hilary. And so, in the heart of a tragedy in stone so old as to be beautiful, she explored for the first time her most secret feelings about that dear, watching presence at Nuns Farthing.

Guardian angel, she had said once to Mrs. Pilton. But if he had lived, if he had come home as she had hoped, and found her there in the house—. He would have been thirty-three—old enough to know all about things, old enough to be depended on, young enough, perhaps, not to think her too much of a kid—. A tingling ran through her taut body. They would have been old friends when they met—well, at least on her side, and even without the strange intimacy of the last few weeks. Perhaps—. Slowly the glory spread. Already she loved him, blindly. Perhaps he would have loved her too. Perhaps they would have been married, and gone on living at Nuns Farthing forever after. . . .

Sitting hunched up on the grassy bank, she hid her face in her arms, crossed on her bent knees, shaken and trembling with new knowledge. She belonged to Hilary. Something had happened to him out in India, but he had come back anyhow, to find her. The joy and pain of it were equal. She belonged to Hilary, and now she had lost him, and her life was over because she could never marry anyone else, and no one would ever understand that it was happiness for them both just to be in the house together. Nobody would ever let them alone. If she went back to Nuns Farthing, to Hilary, she would only be sent off to Switzerland. Whichever way she turned, there was no way clear to him now. And he was the man she was born to love. . . .

It would be so simple, if only people would not interfere. All she wanted was to be allowed to go on as she was. Years at Nuns Farthing would pass swiftly and peacefully. The garden would get more beautiful with tending, and there were books in the house to last a lifetime. Gradually she would have become a middle-aged spinster, living contentedly between garden and library, with a descendant of Muffin's in attendance, popular with the village children because she gave them sweets and let them picnic on the lawn and carry away all the flowers they liked. She would have been a nice old maid, she thought, not lonely and cross and unhappy like some, because there would always be Hilary. Surely it wasn't such an unreasonable thing to ask, just to grow old gently in a house nobody else cared to live in. . . .

Nuns Farthing. She contemplated its name curiously. There had been a convent once, she supposed—the home of other women who for one reason or another hadn't felt equal to the world and only wanted to be left alone. It used to be quite a common thing, hundreds of years ago, for a woman who had lost her lover to become a nun. Even Guinevere, at the end, had found peace that way, renouncing Lancelot. There must still be places nowadays where you could go and be a nun. Switzerland—

there must be convent schools in Switzerland—if once she could get to a place like that she could make the nuns understand, and then they would let her stay with them in peace. . . .

She had no idea how long she sat there, with her face hidden in her arms. When she raised her head at last it was because there had come stealing across the grass on the still air, the faint, sweet drift of incense. She gazed round her slowly, at the crumbling walls and jagged arches, and the empty window-frames, which had not seen a service in three hundred years. But Sabrina sat there, strangely comforted, with the smell of ghostly incense in her nostrils.

The shadows stretched long across the grassy nave now, and the air was getting chilly. Sabrina realized that she was hungry, and it was nearly dinner time. She rose and shook out her coat and collected her dressing-case and put her hat right. That day last spring she and Aunt Effie had lunched at the Pilgrim Inn in the square. She would get dinner there, and take a room for the night, and perhaps in the morning she could decide what to do. Perhaps she would ask if they needed any extra help at the inn, and earn her keep. She would like to stay here for a little while, quietly, and think things out. She could post a letter to Aunt Effie from Wells, to say that she was all right. And she would not sign her real name in the hotel register. . . .

XIX

THEY missed her at Nuns Farthing, of course, by tea time. Hilary heard them calling her in the garden, in the passage, and began to wonder too. At five o'clock Mrs. Pilton came up and looked in at his door, to see if Sabrina had fallen asleep up there. With one inscrutable glance round the empty room, she closed the door and went away again.

A little later he went out and sat on his stairs, listening. He was by no means as alarmed as Aunt Effie, with Switzerland on her guilty conscience, but he wanted to keep track of things. While he sat there, shamelessly waiting to eavesdrop, Aunt Effie came upstairs and went into Sabrina's room. In a few minutes she came out again and hurried downstairs towards the study. Hilary followed to the top of the lower flight.

"Alan! Alan!" cried Aunt Effie at the study door. "Her dressing-case is gone, and her toilet things! She packed them up! She's run away! *Now* will you ring up the police at Wells and give them a description?"

Father's reply was inaudible to Hilary at the top of the stairs.

"Well, you'd better ring them up first and get them

started on it. Say we'll be there directly after dinner. I'll go and bring the car round now."

Again Father was inaudible.

"Why, just tell them what she looks like and how old she is and when she was last seen!" said Aunt Effie impatiently. "You ought to know as much as *that* about your own daughter! She was wearing a blue dress and she took her tan-colored coat."

Packed a bag and bolted, wondered Hilary, beginning to be concerned. Something on her mind. Something for which Aunt Effie was probably to blame.

He hung about the stairhead while they ate a hasty and unhappy meal, and before they had finished he ran down through the lower hall and got into the rumble seat of the waiting car. Whatever it was, he meant to be in on it from now on. He had no intention of sitting at home while they chivvied Sabrina round the countryside.

In a few minutes they came out, accompanied by Bella, who eyed the car with aversion and went off into fits of shrill yapping. Aunt Effie was distressed and inclined to argue with her.

"Oh, leave the dog at home, for heaven's sake!" said Father furiously, from his seat in front.

"But usually she *likes* to ride, Alan! I can't *think* what makes her act this way!"

"It's hysterical," said Father conclusively. "Probably needs to go to the vet. Do come along, Effie, we shall be all night at this rate!"

Very unwillingly Aunt Effie took her place behind the wheel, and they drove away, leaving Bella outraged and shrieking in the driveway.

The hood was down, and fragments of their conversation floated back to Hilary on the road. Aunt Effie blamed herself for not leading up more persuasively to the matter of the school in Switzerland, and reiterated her intention to get Sabrina out of the house as soon as possible. Hilary was enlightened. Threatened with school against her will, Sabrina had run away. Perfectly natural. Just what she expected ultimately to accomplish by that rather childish form of protest he couldn't see, and he doubted if she could either. Running away is something practically everybody does at least once in a lifetime. Usually one merely arrives back, sadder and wiser, at the starting point. He had not much doubt that Sabrina would be found quite safe, but he meant to go into the matter himself, in case they overlooked anything.

The idea of Sabrina in a girls' school in Switzerland certainly did not appeal to him. She had come to depend on him now, and she would be miserable without him, he knew. But they were trying to take her away from him. He could follow her, he supposed, wherever they chose to send her, whatever they chose to do—but he found the prospect both difficult and embarrassing. The intricacies of a school régime were enough to tree him entirely. Nor could he contemplate without serious qualms any length of time in the narrow confines of a London flat which would be shared by Bella.

It had been fairly easy, so far, but what was to become of them now? So far as he himself was concerned, he could hang about in the streets until she came out and get a sight of her that way now and then, just to make sure she was well and reasonably happy. It would be fantastically like carrying on some sort of intrigue. He recalled one or two episodes in his very early youth, with unsatisfactory meetings snatched in parks and tea-shops, robbed of all intimacy and leisure, making for misunderstandings and quarrels. At least Sabrina wouldn't quarrel with him. But the thing she needed from him, a sense of peaceful companionship, would be impossible away from Nuns Farthing.

He perceived that Aunt Effie was running on about alternative remedies, such as a trip to Brittany, *en famille*—to which Father objected instantly that he couldn't get away—or a month at the seaside somewhere in England, just Sabrina and herself, and of course Bella. "I don't think you realize, Alan, that girls at that age are very serious problems. Has it occurred to you that she might work herself up into nervous prostration?" "*I* shall get nervous prostration," interposed Father regrettably, "if you don't keep an eye on the road!"

For the first time Hilary was visited by alarming doubts, as he contemplated Sabrina's future. For the first time he saw himself at war with the world for her future, and he saw that it wouldn't do. These people might be stupid and criminally negligent, but they meant well, and they were her only actual bulwarks against life. Drive them to desperate measures, and where would it end? For the first time he wondered if it would have been better for her if he had never come back at all. Not that he had had much choice . . .

The police station at Wells was only mildly concerned about Sabrina's mysterious disappearance. They took the viewpoint that a girl of nearly eighteen who had calmly packed a bag and walked out in broad daylight with at least two pounds in her purse was not in any immediate danger. They were pretty sure that she had not been seen at the railway station and she was not at any of the hotels, but they were making further inquiries and would probably have something to report in the morning. They advised Aunt Effie to go home and get some rest and be prepared to come and collect the girl when she turned up safe and sound the next day. In fact, they suggested, she might be turning up at home any minute now, none the worse for her adventure, and it would be a pity if there was no one there to receive her.

Baffled and silenced by the bland efficiency of the law, Aunt Effie and Father returned to the car and drove away in the direction of Nuns Farthing. But without Hilary. He was far from satisfied, and he meant to drift round the railway station and a bar or two, picking up local gossip.

He went first to the Swan, which was probably the

only hotel Sabrina was likely to know about in Wells, and when the manageress' back was turned he inspected the register, but without success. He glanced into the dining-room and the lounge and as he expected drew blank. He then went down the road and the social scale and finally fetched up in a pub bar where a dart game was in progress.

Various ancients had grown gregarious over their mild and bitter, and the entry of a constable just come off duty was greeted with a small stir. Had the missing young lady been found, they wanted to know. No, she had not.

"I saw un, I did," volunteered an old boy in the corner with a bubbling pipe.

"Aye, Tom, 'ere, *'e* saw un," asserted his companion proudly.

"Did you, now?" said the constable, humoring them. "Where would that be?"

"Pretty creetur she were, too," mumbled the old man into his beer. "Nigh broke her neck, she did, gettin' on the bus."

"*What bus?*" said Hilary involuntarily, drawing nearer.

"How do you know so much about it?" inquired the constable, cagily.

" 'Erbert, 'ere, were down at the railway station. 'E 'eard 'em asking about people takin' tickets fer London an' that. *I* said, 'No London in it,' I said. 'She took the bus fer Glastonbury,' I said. So 'Erbert said—"

"What makes you think it was the same young lady that's missing?" inquired the constable, receiving his pint with a wink at the barmaid, who leaned her elbows on the counter to hear.

"Not local stuff, she weren't," said old Tom sagely. "A mite too thin, and that. One o' they London diets, I shouldn't wonder," continued the old man, pretending not to notice the flattering silence which had fallen on the room. "An' luggin' a great 'eavy bag like that, and runnin' arter the bus, all dazed like, arter lookin' right at it, you might say, without movin' 'and or foot till it was just about too late. She'd a-gone flat on her face on the step, she would, if young Jessop 'adn't caught 'er arm and drug 'er up inside. Gave 'im a fright, too, I can tell you!"

"When was all this, Tom?" The constable was interested now.

"When I was a-standin' down in the square watchin' of the buses, like I always do, 'long about noon time today."

"It might be the one, at that," said the constable, and drained his tankard. "I'll go along and tell 'em at the station, before they close. They might make something out of it. How was she dressed, this girl you saw?"

"Might be somethin' blue," said old Tom with nonchalance, and buried his face in his beer. "Pretty creetur," he added, half emerging. "But wants fattenin'—nothin' to get a man's bed warm o' nights, he, he, he—" He disappeared again, into his beer.

"Blue," said the constable. "That's right. Carrying a bag. Glastonbury bus. Well, no harm in letting them know at the station."

But Hilary had slipped out the door ahead of him and was hurrying towards the square where the last bus for Glastonbury was loading. He waited on the curb till its gears went home, and then swung on through the open back door and dropped into a seat near the rear. I really must solve this transportation problem, he thought. There must be some way to get about without all this trouble.

It was quite dark when they got to Glastonbury, and the Pilgrim Inn was dim and quiet. He walked into the deserted hall, and with a quick glance round stepped into the office and sought the register. The last signature of the day amused him. *Mary Smith*, he read, and beside it, *No. 27*.

Still smiling, he went upstairs and found the number on a door and listened. Not a sound. He walked through the painted wooden panels. The room was dark, except for a glimmer from the window where the curtains had been drawn back to admit the first morning light. Sabrina was asleep in the tumbled bed, one fragile arm outflung.

He bent above her with mingled thankfulness and anxiety, and her troubled face relaxed. She stirred a little, and settled more comfortably into the pillow. Very cautiously he straightened the covers and drew them over her. Sabrina smiled in her sleep, and as she did so he knew again the swift sweet thrill of elation which had surprised him only the day before while she drank her tea on the side of the bed. He retreated in all humility and gratitude to a rather uncomfortable-looking chair by the window, rested his crossed feet on the bureau, and took up his vigil.

He had found her, and she was safe, but what came next? An alarming sense of his own helplessness was growing on him tonight. Whatever happened, he could only stand by and watch. But from now on, he dared not let her out of his sight. Suppose he lost her. It came as rather a shock to him that he had not, apparently, developed any sort of second sight which would guide him to her again, across the world. If once he lost touch with her, or at least with the family, it might be years before he saw her again . . . centuries. . . .

But she needed him. He was so sure of that. She belonged to him. It was his job to look after her. But how?

Someone was ringing the night bell, and banging on the street door. There was a stir downstairs. Sabrina slept through it, smiling.

Arrival of distraught family, thought Hilary. Let her have her sleep out, why can't you? Go to bed and shut up till morning.

There was a tapping on Sabrina's door, and she sat up, startled.

"*It's all right,*" he said gently. "*They left the bloodhound at home.*"

"Who's there?" called Sabrina tremulously.

"It's me, dear—Aunt Effie. Open the door."

"*You might as well let her get it over,*" Hilary advised, preparing to surrender his chair.

Sabrina got out of bed and snapped on the light and unlocked the door.

"You naughty girl, how *could* you worry us so? We had to ring up the police station at Wells!" Aunt Effie came in and shut the door behind her.

"I'm sorry." Sabrina returned to the bed and sat up in the middle of it with the covers pulled round her, looking very small and forlorn.

"Somebody saw you getting on the bus for Glastonbury, or I really don't know what we should have done, we might have worried all night long—"

"I'm sorry, Auntie. I meant to post you a letter in the morning to say I was all right."

"But what were you going to *do*, dear, out in the world all alone?"

"I don't know—I thought of trying to get a job—"

"A *job!*" cried Aunt Effie, as though she had said a rattlesnake.

"Well, I only had two pounds seven, and so—"

"But surely you meant to come back home tomorrow!"

"No."

"But *why?* Your father thinks it's all because you didn't want to go to a school, but surely—"

"I didn't want to leave Nuns Farthing."

"But you did leave it, when you came here!" Aunt Effie pointed out triumphantly.

"I know. I was wrong."

"Well, I'm glad you see that now, at least. Sabrina, darling, promise me you'll never run away again!" But Sabrina was silent, her arms locked round her bent knees, staring at the foot of the bed. "And I'll make you a promise too," Aunt Effie hurried on persuasively. "I'll promise not to say anything more about Switzerland, unless you decide you really want to go. Is that a bargain?"

Sabrina turned a faintly hopeful face towards her aunt.

"Do you mean that, Auntie?"

"Of course I do! If I'd any idea you felt as strongly as all this about not going—well, we just won't say anything more about it, shall we! No more school—no more running away!"

"That's not good enough, Sabrina," Hilary warned her. *"Make her promise you won't have to leave Nuns Farthing."*

But Sabrina, heavy with exhaustion, and being naturally a trustful soul, saw only that her lifelong dread of school could be forever dispelled.

"I promise," she said.

"And *I* promise!" said Aunt Effie brightly. "Now, your father and I have taken rooms here for the rest of the night and we'll all drive home together in the morning. Just think, your father has gone to bed in a room marked *Henry VIII*, isn't that funny? And there are two lovely beds in my room, wouldn't you like to come in there and be cozy?"

"No, thank you, Aunt Effie. I've unpacked here."

"You're sure you wouldn't like me to help you move your things in there with me?"

"No, thank you, Auntie."

"Well, remember, now, you've promised."

"Yes, Auntie. Good-night."

"Good-night, dear. Shall I put out the light?"

"Yes, please."

Aunt Effie kissed her affectionately, and snapped out the light, and went away. Sabrina got up to lock the door behind her, and crawled back into bed and pulled the covers well up over her head.

Hilary restored his feet to the bureau and settled back to think. He knew as well as anything that Aunt Effie's crafty bargain still left the way open for her to take Sabrina away from Nuns Farthing as soon as she chose, and he was sure that she would lose no time about it now, unless—

He contemplated the only answer in the world. If Aunt Effie could somehow be convinced that he was no longer in the house—. But merely for him to keep still and not upset Bella was not enough. If he could somehow exorcise himself publicly from Nuns Farthing, Sabrina might be allowed to stay on there in peace.

XX

BY taking the earliest possible bus next morning, grumbling to himself because he had not yet evolved a disembodied transit system, Hilary arrived home before the others, who traveled by car after breakfast.

When Sabrina ran up to his room he was already there, and it never occurred to her that he had left it. He could tell by her face that last night's false security still existed, and that she thought herself safe, not only from Switzerland but from having to leave Nuns Farthing. He wondered how long that would last.

Father gave it away at luncheon, by announcing that he had arranged to take rooms in Wells for the next month at least, instead of going up to Town with them tomorrow.

"Tomorrow!" said Sabrina incredulously.

"I shall be able to use the Wells Museum then, until my book is ready for the printer," Father explained.

"But you said I didn't have to go!" cried Sabrina. "Aunt Effie, you promised!"

"I promised about Switzerland," Aunt Effie conceded cautiously. "But when I thought you *were* going, I made arrangements to give up the lease here."

"When?"

"This week."

"But—" Sabrina looked blankly from one to the other. "Where are we going to live?"

"Where we have always lived—in the flat in Town," said Father. "That is, I shall rejoin you there in a few weeks."

"Does that mean we're leaving this house forever?"

"Forever?" Father considered the melodramatic word critically. "Why, yes, I suppose it amounts to that."

"I wasn't going to tell you just yet," admitted Aunt Effie. "Not until you were rested, that is, but now that you know, you might as well start your packing directly after luncheon. I thought with luck we might catch the nine o'clock train in the morning. Your father wants the car left here, of course."

Sabrina saw that she had been tricked and beaten, sensed treachery somewhere, but was too dazed to lay her finger on it.

"You mean—catch a train for London?" she asked stupidly.

"Well, yes, London first. It will be rather nice, don't you think, to see the shops again, and go to a big cinema?"

"Then it's over," said Sabrina hopelessly, not looking at them. "I've lost it—forever."

"What, dear? We thought of looking up places at the seashore for a month later on. Just you and me and Bella, you'd like that, wouldn't you! Do you remember that funny place in Wales we went to one time when you were a very little girl? I never could pronounce its funny name, but we had lodgings looking right out over the water, and you used to have a little bucket and spade and dig in the sand."

"That Swiss school," said Sabrina, looking down at her plate. "Was it a convent?"

"Why—no," said Aunt Effie, with a glance at Father. "But it's very odd that you should ask, because your father did say he thought convent schools sounded very pretty."

"I was thinking it must be nice to be a nun," said Sabrina simply, as though talking to herself.

"*What?*" said Father, so that Aunt Effie jumped and dropped her fork. "Now, look here, Sabrina, I won't have any religious nonsense, do you understand? A fellow you've never seen goes and dies out in India and you want to be a nun! That's nonsense. You're going to forget all about it at once—forget this house and everything in it!"

"Really, Alan, I don't think—"

"I don't mean to be harsh or unreasonable," he added more quietly, smitten by her smallness and whiteness, so motionless in her chair. "But I expect my daughter to grow up into a sane, healthy-minded woman, with the right ideas about marriage and children. There's no reason on earth why I shouldn't see you married to some decent fellow and safely a mother before I die."

Sabrina stared at him in dumb incredulity. Married?

To someone who wasn't Hilary? Children—that weren't Hilary's? Could they never understand that she belonged to him?

"Well, I wouldn't go as far as all that, Alan!" cried Aunt Effie, with her gay, silly laugh, and she reached to lay a protective hand on Sabrina's, where it rested on the edge of the table. "Not necessarily, I mean! We spinsters lead the happiest lives, when all's said and done! Fewer worries and responsibilities, I always think—though some of us *have* got darling nieces who make us a great deal of extra bother, haven't we!" She patted Sabrina's hand. "There's certainly no need to rush her off into *marriage*, Alan, I assure you! She could do far worse than jog along comfortably like her old auntie!"

Sabrina blinked down at Aunt Effie's hand on hers—brown, knobby, coarsened, with short thick nails pale against the tanned skin. And then as her father spoke again she turned her head slowly to look at him—scraggy and dry and opinionated, speaking of marriage as though it was something you ordered by post from Selfridge's. Jog along alone—and forgetful—and complaisant. Get irritable, or silly, or futile. Grow old—like *these?*

"Some chap with eyes in his head is bound to turn up soon enough, I dare say," Father was assuring Aunt Effie obstinately. "The child is very like her mother, and Joan was a dashed pretty girl when I married her."

"Was she happy with you?" asked Sabrina in the dead silence which enveloped his final word.

"Naturally she was," said Father, without hesitation,

but his eyes as they rested on his daughter were guarded and hostile and bleak. "Why shouldn't she have been?"

"Then why did she die?" queried Sabrina unreasonably, and there was a small gasp from Aunt Effie at the other end of the table.

"Because she had a fall just before you were born," he stated with brutal simplicity. "You were born too soon. It killed her."

"Alan—!" Aunt Effie faltered into silence as that bleak, angry gaze came round to her.

"Sabrina is old enough to know these things," he asserted. "You should have told her long ago."

"She—she never asked me—"

But now he seemed to have forgotten them both, looking inward unwillingly at the cold cinders of an old, unhappy passion, and at an old sorrow, bitter and unresigned.

"They could have saved her," he was saying, and his face as they stared at him was savage and strange. "It was her life or the child's, they said. I told them which it was to be, and the fools did as they pleased—they needn't have let her die—I begged them not to let her die—"

"Oh, Alan—!" breathed Aunt Effie, sadly, and her foolish, pretty face was puckered with pity as she sat looking at him across the table. "Oh, Alan, I thought—" She thought he had forgotten, after all these years of his coldness and absentmindedness. She hoped even now that he would not remember the surprising words of the young doctor who had been left behind by the specialist to fight the losing battle for Joan's life. "She isn't *trying!*" cried the young doctor in despair. "She won't *help* me—!" Even now, Aunt Effie was not sure that Joan might not have been happy if she had lived—that is, Joan might have outgrown her odd, timid ways that seemed almost as though she was—well, *afraid* of Alan, or possibly didn't really *like* him, when anyone could see the poor man wouldn't hurt a fly, and surely a sister ought to know. . . .

"Doctors! Pigheaded, blundering fools!" said Father, and hid himself abruptly behind the *Times*. "Always think they know best!"

Sabrina left the table without a word, and went to her room and sat down there, sick and cold and faint. Her face felt rigid and drawn, as though she had never smiled, and never would again, yet her teeth were chattering behind tight-pressed lips and her eyeballs burned like coals.

Muffin came and got into her lap, digging in his claws, but she took no notice of him. He seemed to belong to someone else, someone she had known once, to whom he had been important and dear. He had no place in the desert where she sat. Life stretched out ahead of her, an unmitigated aeon of ugliness. Perhaps after a while you got numb, and didn't mind anything. . . .

When Aunt Effie came up at tea time, bringing a large suitcase, Sabrina rose mechanically and began as requested to fill it with the contents of the chest of drawers.

Aunt Effie noticed with relief that at least she wasn't crying, and went away again, more or less on tiptoe.

Sabrina went down to dinner when she was called, and sat through the meal in silence, staring at her plate, deaf to remonstrances. After dinner she went back to her room and began to walk up and down the floor aimlessly, her hands locked together. It was no good going up to Hilary now, she told herself. Under the pressure of her immediate misery, the contented hours she had spent in his company seemed completely unreal, and as distant as a dream. Like Muffin, Hilary had happened to somebody else, somebody who wasn't here any more, somebody she had lost.

About ten o'clock Aunt Effie looked in at the door and advised her to get a good sleep, as they had to be up early tomorrow. Obediently Sabrina undressed and got into bed, where she lay with wide open eyes, watching the slow summer dark close in on the window. The night passed in a half-waking nightmare in which the Swiss school got mixed up with the Spanish civil war, and nuns were made to goose-step, and the ceiling of the dormitory fell in, and lastly she saw someone lying dead face down in a red pool of blood, and though she knelt beside him in terror she could not lift him enough to see his face, but she knew it was Hilary, and that he was really gone this time, entirely gone, and the world was empty of him—and then she woke.

It was seven o'clock. She reached for her dressing-gown and slippers, possessed once more by the old unreasoning need of Hilary's own four walls—sanctuary—refuge from nightmare.

But Aunt Effie knocked on the door and showed a determinedly smiling face at the widening crack.

"Oh, you're awake!" she commented brightly. "That's good! Breakfast in half an hour. Get your things all ready to close the bags before you come down, won't you."

She disappeared.

It was no use. Nothing was any use any more. Doggedly Sabrina washed her face and brushed her hair and dressed herself, and laid her toilet things and nightgown away in the dressing-case, and went down to breakfast. Her head felt very hot and much too big, her hands were icy, and her knees wobbled. All her will-power was in her stoic silence throughout that awful meal, while she sat dry-eyed, choking down a cup of hot tea. It was no good behaving like a baby, making scenes. And she mustn't look a fright with crying when she went up to tell Hilary good-by. . . .

When Father and Aunt Effie rose from the breakfast table she rose too and climbed the two flights to Hilary's room shakily, holding to the bannisters all the way.

XXI

HILARY had been pondering the matter of self-exorcism, and arriving nowhere. At last he consulted the dictionary without much hope.

"Exorcise: to clear (a person or place) of evil spirits; to purify or set free from malignant influences," he read. And as an example, a quotation from Lytton's *Harold:* "Muttering hymns, monks huddled together . . . as if to exorcise the land of a demon."

All this rather hurt his feelings and got him no further. Evil he was not, nor malignant. He objected to the word "demon." Obviously, "exorcise" was the wrong term.

But the idea was growing on him that Sabrina, since she was making herself ill and unhappy, must be encouraged to get clear of the whole thing, including himself, if she could, at least for a time. He had decided not to attempt to interfere with her departure, nor influence her to continue her futile fight to be near him. This meant loneliness and readjustment of his days at Nuns Farthing, but he felt it would be best for her.

It was an added irony, it seemed to him, that they should have to say good-by just now, on what might have been the very day of their first meeting on his proposed mid-August return. It was hard to give her up to whatever life had in store for her, without him, at perhaps the exact point in time when he should have received her whole future into his own keeping—for he was sure now that if once he had come to Nuns Farthing as he was meant to come, on some mortal errand, he would have known her for his own and arranged his career accordingly. Not for Sabrina the hardy existence of a Frontier wife, as Alice might have been expected to face it. He would have resigned, for Sabrina, and built a life in England. He would have settled down, perhaps a little incredulously at first, in some niche at Whitehall, with long country week-ends at Nuns Farthing. He knew very well that he could have been useful at Whitehall, to the men who did not know what he already knew at first hand. He would have kept Sabrina safe. . . .

Daydreams. Ghostly dreams of a happiness he had missed by a hair's breadth of time, on some unfathomable miscalculation, while an obstinate, unswerving destiny still labored to bring them together. He felt that he stood on the edge of dizzying mysteries. She was his, but he was dead, and so today he would have to see her go from him, powerless to interfere even if he had dared. And he did not dare.

Conceivably, she would find her own way back to him some day. By then, the house would have a bad name—he would see to that—and they would be allowed to have it to themselves. A long, long wait for him, perhaps;

years of unmeasured time in endless solitude. Presumably he would grow no older. And she? Sabrina—old?

Suddenly he was more afraid for Sabrina than he had ever been for himself in a perilous lifetime. What was ahead for her? Where would she turn in her loneliness and confusion? They would encourage her to marry some fool like George or like her father. She would be frightened—she would not understand—she would not know that he was waiting—she would make mistakes and be miserable. . . .

The same sort of panic he had known that night at the club, when he heard his own death announced by Denby, welled up in him again, so that he beat frantically against the invisible barriers of his own helplessness. Anything could happen to Sabrina now, and he was powerless even to catch her tears on his lips. It set him pacing the floor, at grips once more with immensities no man should have to face. Sabrina, setting out alone into the world again, lost, betrayed, and bewildered. And he had to let her go. There was no way to keep her here, and he had no right to try. Oh, God, keep her safe—you meant her to be safe. . . .

He heard her feet on the stairs.

An early morning reconnaissance had shown him that departure was imminent, but he was not quite prepared for her stricken look and feverish eyes, now that she stood leaning against the closed door as though she had no strength left to stand alone.

"*But you haven't lost me, you know,*" he told her reasonably, like a man who puts aside his own anxieties to soothe a sick child. "*I've been reading luggage labels, I know exactly where you'll be in London. I'll keep track of things, always. We won't end like this. I don't know yet what happens, but this isn't the end, you can be sure of that—*"

White-faced, silent, gallant in her tearlessness, she came on into the room and, starting at the mantelpiece, began to tend it for the last time; picked a fallen rose petal from beneath the vase on the mantelshelf—with her handkerchief wiped an imaginary speck of dust from a silver candlestick—straightened the silk cushion in the chair where the book about ghosts had lain—adjusted a fold of the curtain beside the sunny window seat where Muffin loved to lie—cast a critical eye over the immaculate polished surface of the desk, setting the blotter true by the fraction of an inch—touched lightly with a caress one of the sphinx book-ends he had thought highly of—moved on into the bedroom end and paused at the tall chest of drawers to face Alice's picture neatly into the room again as it had been in the beginning. And as she turned away towards the bedside table her eyes fell on the collar box beside the silver frame.

The collar box.

Her mind flew back to the day of the treasure hunt, when the loose catch had first tempted her exploring fingers—winged collars for evening wear—and in the center space something small and black and cold, like a snake. . . .

"Sabrina," said Hilary apprehensively, watching from across the room.

She stretched out both hands to the collar box, drew it forward to the edge, and opened the lid. A shiver ran through her as she saw again the little black gun in its nest. To think she had almost forgotten it, when perhaps it was the answer to everything. Perhaps that was why it was here. Surely if she died now, here in the room, Hilary's arms would close round her at last. And then she needn't leave him—ever. . . .

"Sabrina, don't touch it—it's loaded—it will go off—"

She laid hold of the handle firmly—cold, like a snake—and lifted the gun out of the box.

"Sabrina, you've got to hear me! Put it back! You've got to go on living—even if you seem to lose touch with me—"

Inevitably her finger found the safety catch and released it with a small click.

"But they're right, Sabrina, I'm not good for you! You'll grow up, you'll live your life, and then, when it's time, we'll be together again. Sabrina—don't—!"

She did not hear him. She had never heard him. She stood looking down at the gun in her hand, fearlessly now, with a sort of curiosity. Slowly the muzzle was turning in towards her body.

Caution, prudence, reason, all left him in a rising terror of losing her forever. Moving instinctively on the split second, as he had done a hundred times in his life before, he lunged across the room and knocked the gun on to the floor by sweeping his hand through hers—so that she was left staring at her empty fingers and at the gun where it lay on the carpet at the edge of the bed.

"Hilary!" she whispered, and her feverish eyes searched the room again minutely, without success.

"I had to stop you," he said apologetically. *"There is some sort of pattern. Don't ever meddle with it."*

She threw out her hands in passionate appeal to the empty room.

"Hilary, wherever you are, you've got to hear me! You've got to come back and help me!"

"I did come back," he said.

"Don't let them do this to me! Don't let them take me away! I'm safe here with you—I'm afraid to go—"

"I know, sweetheart—I know."

"Afraid, afraid, Hilary, can't you hear? Dreadful things can't happen to me here—please let me stay!"

"Not like that, Sabrina—that won't help."

"Answer me, Hilary, you must answer! What will become of me if I leave this house? I might never feel as though you were in the same room with me again! I might get ill and die, alone! Or I might have to live till I'm eighty, without you near! Hilary, promise me that when I die you'll be there!"

"Yes, my darling, yes—I will be there."

"You don't answer," she said hopelessly, and put both hands to her throbbing temples. "I can't hear you. You won't help me. What shall I do?"

Aunt Effie's voice, too bright, too brisk, too firmly implying that all was right with the world, floated up the stairs.

"Sabrina! We're waiting!"

"What shall I do?" she said again, between her hands.

There was no answer he could give but silence. He withdrew backwards to the window seat, moving with infinite care, and sat down there remotely, striving now to eradicate himself from her consciousness after that one moment's reckless contact. He had done all he could, he did not dare do more. There were no short cuts, he had shown her that. If he did not answer, did not stir, perhaps she would resign herself to the lack of communication between them and go quickly now, relieving the strain their parting put upon her. She was young, and had not learned fatalism. The very young never can. But the sooner she realized that there is a point beyond which it is no good resisting the trend of events, the easier it would be for her.

And so he deserted her utterly, for her own good, and she felt his going, and gazed about her a moment longer forlornly. She went to the desk and picked up his little brown pipe with caressing fingers.

"Could I take this with me?" she asked, and waited hopelessly for his reply. "Hilary—please?"

But he sat very still on the window seat, cutting himself off from her deliberately. It was best for her not to take anything with her which would bind her to him in any way. She must have every chance now, for the usual sort of life, without him. She must be free, to forget him and their strange companionship if she could.

Aunt Effie called again, from the foot of the stairs. "Sabrina! Your father's in a hurry!"

With a sigh, she replaced the pipe on the desk and left the room empty-handed, drooping, numbed with despair.

A docile automaton, she collected her hat and coat and bag at Aunt Effie's bidding and went down to where the car was waiting outside the front door. Bareheaded, with her coat over her arm, she climbed obediently into the rumble seat with the suitcases, heard Aunt Effie making bright farewells to Mrs. Pilton, heard minute directions given by her father regarding the despatch of his luggage to the lodgings in Wells, heard her own voice asking Mrs. Pilton to please be kind to Muffin.

The car started with a jerk. She did not look back at Hilary's windows, but sat stolidly clutching her hat and coat and staring straight ahead as they rolled down the drive.

The big black limousine driven by a uniformed chauffeur was coming from the left, much too fast for so narrow a lane. Aunt Effie's wide and always uncertain turn out of the gate to the left covered much more than her half of the road, just where the branches of the old oak overhung the hedge. There was a blast of the limousine's horn, a grinding of brakes, a thudding crash, and then a sharp, snapped-off scream.

The nose of the big limousine was jammed into the side of the smaller car, which was tilted at a crazy angle with two wheels clear of the ground. The chauffeur, who was merely shaken up a little and whose glass was all intact, jumped out and ran, white-faced, to where Sabrina had been thrown clear, into the ditch.

She lay very still, face down. As he turned her over and raised her in his arms, Mrs. Pilton came running down the drive, and Father limped towards them, dabbing with his handkerchief at a long cut in his cheek from the broken windscreen. Aunt Effie had quietly fainted behind the wheel, and Bella was up on the seat beside her, whimpering and trying to lick her face.

Father stood staring down at the chauffeur's quiet burden.

"She was in the back," he was saying in a dazed, apologetic sort of way. "There was nothing for her to hold to—she must have been shot out on her head. Is she all right?" He peered suddenly into the man's rigid face, in growing apprehension. "Is she all right?" he insisted.

"I—don't know," said the chauffeur between stiff lips. "I—can't be sure."

"Hilary—Hilary, where are you?" She had reached the second flight of stairs already, on her way to him. *"Hilary, something's happened—I don't have to go, after all—"*

Then she saw him.

. . . .

A generation from now, on a summer day, three village children will come along the lane and pause at the sagging gate of Nuns Farthing, gazing in at the riot of untended bloom which was once the herbaceous border. And one of them, a visiting cousin from the next county, will express a desire to pilfer such lovely flowers, all going to waste on an empty house where the window glass is latticed by uncut tendrils of Virginia creeper, where a top-floor shutter is flung wide to the sunlight, and the casement stands open in the June heat.

"Come away, Mildred, do!" the others will advise her in lowered tones, dragging her back from the weed-grown drive into the lane again. "We never go there—it's *haunted!*"